Mrs. Stevens hears the mermaids singing

BOOKS BY MAY SARTON

POETRY
Encounter in April
Inner Landscape
The Lion and the Rose
The Land of Silence
In Time like Air
Cloud, Stone, Sun, Vine
A Private Mythology
As Does New Hampshire
A Grain of Mustard Seed
A Durable Fire
Collected Poems, 1930–1973
Selected Poems of May Sarton
   (edited by Serena Sue
   Hilsinger and Lois Byrnes)
Halfway to Silence
Letters from Maine
The Silence Now
Colleced Poems 1930–1993
Coming into Eighty
Catching Beauty: The
   Earliest Poems (edited by
   Susan Sherman)

NOVELS
The Single Hound
The Bridge of Years
Shadow of a Man
A Shower of Summer Days
Faithful Are the Wounds
The Birth of a Grandfather
The Fur Person
The Small Room
Joanna and Ulysses
Mrs. Stevens Hears the
   Mermaids Singing
Miss Pickthorn and Mr. Hare
The Poet and the Donkey
Kinds of Love
As We Are Now
Cruel Conversations
A Reckoning
Anger
The Magnificent Spinster
The Education of Harriet
   Hatfield

NONFICTION
I Knew a Phoenix
Plant Dreaming Deep
Journal of a Solitude
A World of Light
The House by the Sea
Recovering: A Journal
At Seventy: A Journal
Honey in the Hive
Among the Usual Days: A
   Portrait (edited by Susan
   Sherman)
After the Stroke: A Journal
Writings on Writing
May Sarton: A Self-Portrait
Endgame: A Journal of the
   Seventy-ninth Year
Encore: A Journal of the
   Eightieth Year
At Eighty-Two: A Journal
At Fifteen: A Journal (edited by
   Susan Sherman)

FOR CHILDREN
Punch's Secret
A Walk through the Woods

ANTHOLOGY

Sarton Selected: An
   Anthology of the Journals,
   Novels, and Poetry (edited
   by Bradford Dudley Daziel)

LETTERS (edited by Susan
   Sherman)

May Sarton: Selected Letters,
   1916–1954
May Sarton: Selected Letters,
   1955–1995
Dear Juliette: Letters of May
   Sarton to Juliette Huxley
Letters to May by Eleanor
   Mabel Sarton

Mrs. Stevens hears the mermaids singing

A NOVEL BY

MAY SARTON

W · W · NORTON & COMPANY

New York · London

Copyright © 1965 by May Sarton

First published as a Norton paperback 1975; reissued 1993.

All rights reserved.

Library of Congress Cataloging in Publication Data

Sarton, May, 1912–
    Mrs. Stevens hears the mermaids singing.

    I.   Title.
PZ3.S249Mi5   [PS3537.A832]   813'.5'2   74-1349
ISBN 978-0-393-30929-4

W. W. Norton & Company, Inc.
500 Fifth Avenue, New York, N.Y. 10110
www.wwnorton.com

W. W. Norton & Company Ltd.
Castle House, 75/76 Wells Street, London W1T 3QT

Printed in the United States of America

7 8 9 0

to THE MUSE

"From love one can only escape at the price of life itself; and no lessening of sorrow is worth exile from that stream of all things human and divine."

Freya Stark

Contents

Mrs. Stevens hears the mermaids singing

Part I: Hilary

Hilary Stevens half opened her eyes, then closed them again. There was some reason to dread this day, although she had taken in that the sun was shining. The soft green silk curtains pulled across the windows created an aqueous light and added to the illusion that she was swimming up into consciousness from deep water: she had had such dreams! Too many people . . . landscapes . . . fading in and out of each other.

"The thing is," she told herself, "that I am badgered by something."

Perhaps if she turned over it would go away.

Instead she was forced awake by the twice-repeated piercing notes of an oriole in the flowering plum just outside her windows. At the same moment the French clock cut through this spontaneous song with its rigid intervals. Six o'clock.

"Old thing, it's high time you pulled yourself together!"

But the other party of the dialogue rebelled, wanted to stay comfortably in bed, wanted to ward off whatever was to be demanded, wanted to be left in peace. Lately Hilary had observed that she seemed to be two distinct entities, at war. There was a hortatory and impatient person who was irritated by her lethargic twin, that one who had to be prodded awake and commanded like a doddering servant and who was getting old, seventy as one counted years.

First things first. The mind must be summoned back, then one might manage to lift oneself out of bed. Hilary closed her eyes and set herself to cope with consciousness. But oh to slip back into that other world, where in her dreams she flew, covered immense distances with ease, and so often came to such beautiful understanding and peace with those ghosts who in reality had represented chiefly anguish. The past had been extraordinarily present all night . . . , she was preparing herself.

"For what?" the doddering servant wished to know.

"The interviewers, you old fool. They are coming this afternoon!"

This realization acted like a pail of water flung in her face, and Hilary found herself cold-awake, standing rather shakily, supporting herself with one hand on the night table. The room around her was in unusual disorder, open cardboard boxes of files standing about and, on the night table, photographs and old letters. Oh dear! She took refuge in the usual actions, those which began every day. She went first to the window and drew back the curtains. There in the distance, seen across granite boulders and an assortment of wild cherry and locust, lay the great quivering expanse of ocean, blue, blue to the slightly paler line at the horizon. There it was, the old sea, the restorer! Hilary drank it down in one swift glance, and then walked over to the bureau and, over the inexorable minute hand of the French clock, looked into her own eyes, shallow and pale in the morning light.

"God, you look awful," she told herself. "Old crone, with hardly a wisp of hair left, and those dewlaps, and those wrinkles." Merciless she was. But there was also the pleasure of recognition. In the mirror she recognized her *self*, her life companion, for better or worse. She looked at this self with compassion this morning, unmercifully prodded and driven as she had been for just under seventy years. The sense of who she was and what she meant about her own personage began to flow back as she ran a comb through the fine childlike hair, hardly gray, and brushed her teeth—her own, and those the dentists had had to provide over the years.

"Damn it!" she said aloud. It meant, in spite of it all, false teeth, falling hair, wrinkles, I am still myself. They haven't got me yet.

They, . . . the enemies. Who were "they" exactly, she asked herself while she put the kettle on, and admired the breakfast tray as she did each morning, resting her eyes on the red cocks painted on the white cup and saucer, the red

[13

linen cloth, the Quimper jam jar with a strawberry for a knob, rejoicing in order and beauty, as if she had not herself arranged it all the night before.

There were moments when Hilary saw life as tending always toward chaos, when it seemed that all one could be asked was just to keep the ashtrays clean, the bed made, the wastebaskets emptied, as if one never got to the real things because of the constant exhausting battle to keep ordinary life from falling apart. She gave orders to the doddering servant about all this, but the old thing was getting slow. . . .

Now, for instance, she had almost forgotten Sirenica in the cellar! Released, the white cat wound herself round Hilary's legs and purred ecstatically, lifting first one paw and then another and stretching it out into the air, giving a single high-pitched mew when she heard the frigidaire door slam and saw her plate being lifted down.

"Who are 'they,' Sirenica?" Hilary asked aloud, but there was no time to make an answer, for it was necessary while the eggs boiled to put the two little turtles into warm water to wake them up; they looked up at her with eyes as cold as her own, then swam wildly about waiting for their disgusting breakfast of mealy worms. Hilary had bought them on an impulse in the five-and-ten. Their coldness was restful; and she delighted in their beauty, like animated pieces of jade. Also it had been rather comforting to read in a turtle book that they might live to be forty, that the absurd creatures would outlive her. Still, any life is in constant peril, and before she knew it, she had taken on another anxiety, worried when they did not eat for a day, found herself involved, trying to imagine what they might enjoy, an hour outdoors in the sun, or a little piece of fish for a change. She gazed down into the bowl intently, now, studying the delicate webbed feet and tiny tails, often kept wound in under the shell. She forgot about her toast. It was cold when she finally buttered it and took the tray upstairs.

Heaven, to get back into bed for this best hour of the day!—the hour when the door between sleep and waking, between conscious and unconscious, was still ajar and Hilary could consider the strange things that welled up through the night, could lie there looking out to sea, and feel energy flow back while she drank two or three strong cups of tea. With the first, she found herself observing Sirenica, who had jumped up on the bed (hoping no doubt there might be bacon this morning), and had settled down to wash her face. It was a long, intricate process; it began with the long rose-petal tongue lapping all around her mouth and chin, up and down and around, at least fifty times. When every taste of fish and every drop of oiliness had been savored, a washcloth paw lifted, to be licked in its turn, then rubbed back of the ears, round the nose, past the strong whiskers. Hilary watched it all as intently as a cat watches a bird: this was something she had never managed to "get down" in a satisfactory form, but she still had hopes.

With her second cup of tea the unfinished dialogue about "they" was resumed, and she lay back on the pillows ruminating. Of course "they" varied a good deal. At one time in her life, "they" had certainly been the critics. Even the accolade on her last book of poems had left a slightly sour taste. She could not help suspecting that it might be a consolation prize, given rather for endurance than achievement. Her distinguished contemporaries had been dying lately, one by one, so it was all very well to be praised for her vitality and intensity, but . . . , anyway Hilary felt it degrading even to consider the critics. "Old fool, *they* are your own demons," she adjured herself, "the never-conquered demons with whom you carry on the struggle for survival against laziness, depression, guilt, and fatigue." She had hit on the only possible answer to the question. It was completely fruitless to quarrel with the world, whereas the quarrel with oneself was occasionally fruitful, and always, she had to admit, interesting. What sort of questions were those interviewers going to ask? It would be exhilarating to be set what Hilary called "real" questions . . . in fact she had agreed to this visitation because it appeared to be a challenge. Hopefully, she might be forced to confront certain things in her own life and in her work that seemed unresolved, and she was just about to consider these prickly matters when she heard a familiar whistle under the window.

"Drat the boy! What does he want?"

She nearly tipped the whole tray over getting out of bed, and of course Sirenica jumped down at once in a huff. Hilary threw an old Japanese kimono over her shoulders and went to the window, peering down into the strong sunlight. The boy teetered there on the stone wall, head bent, his whole figure betraying unease. She could guess, though she could not see it, that the face under the shock of tow hair, was frowning.

"What is it?" Hilary shouted. "It's the day, you know. You might have let me have my breakfast in peace!"

"What day?"

"The day the interviewers are coming!"

"That's not till four." Now he looked straight up, and she saw something in that face she thought she knew by heart, something she had never seen before.

"Up all night, I suppose." What was it? She asked herself, trying to probe the sullen shadowed eyes looking up at her.

"I've got to see you, Hilary. Just a half hour!"

"Oh all right, come back in an hour or so. Give me time to pull myself together."

He was gone before she closed the window, off and away, while Hilary stood there wondering what sort of night he had spent? Curiously enough she sensed some affinity with her own night of troubled dreams after her long vigil raking up the past—the effect, at least, was the same, for Mar looked exactly as she felt, dissipated, ruffled, a seabird who has been battered by wind, whose wings are stuck with flotsam and jetsam, oil, tar, God knows what.

"Trapped by life," Hilary muttered. She almost fell on one of the cardboard boxes. Oh dear, the morning which had begun rather well, all things considered, was already disintegrating into confusion. Back in bed, she leaned her head against the pillows so she could look at the appeasing ocean and forget all that stuff on the floor . . . , but she could not really rest. She must hurry up if she was to be ready for Mar. Trapped by life. There was, even at seventy, no escape. One did one's work against a steady barrage of demands, of people . . . and the garden too! (It was high time she thought about sowing seeds.) It was all very well to insist that art was art and had no sex, but the fact was that the days of men were not in the same way fragmented, atomized by indefinite small tasks. There was such a thing as woman's work and it consisted chiefly, Hilary sometimes thought, in being able to stand constant interruption and keep your temper. Each single day she fought a war to get to her desk before her little bundle of energy had been dissipated, to push aside or cut through an intricate web of slight threads pulling her in a thousand directions—that unanswered letter, that telephone call, or Mar. It really was not fair of Mar to come this morning with his load of intensity, his deep-set blue eyes, his grief. Oh, she had recognized him all right, the very first day when he turned up to ask if he could moor his boat off her dock!

"In exchange for what?" she had asked, testing him. She was sick and tired of the expectations of the young, that they had rights and all must be done for them, with no return.

Mar had half shut his eyes, ducked his head, and made no answer.

"I need someone to dig up flower beds, spread manure, bring in wood," she said sharply as if it made her cross. "I used to do those things myself, but lately I have found it cuts into my work, don't you know? I get tired. So?"

"I don't like doing any of those things," he had said, "but if you need someone, I guess I'll have to!" He had looked down at her from his spindling height in a rather fatherly way, and Hilary felt herself being tamed.

"Who are you, anyway?"

"Mar. Mar Hemmer." He kicked a pebble with one sneakered foot, no longer fatherly, troubled by her probing gaze. Now she remembered. Why, she knew the boy! "Old Mar Hemmer's grandson, of course!"

Cape Ann used to be full of these tow-headed Finns who came over in the days when the big stone piers berthed sailing ships that carried granite round the world; now the place was a honeycomb of abandoned quarries, many of them deep lakes, taken over by summer people for swimming naked in. The Finns had gone into factories. Yes, it appeared that Mar was living with his grandfather; that was all she learned that day. The facts came later; she had recognized at once her own kind, conflicted, nervous, driven, violent, affectionate. . . . Hilary had read all this in his shy glance and guessed at some trouble. Well, she could use a boy round the place, and she knew herself well enough to accept that anyone she took in would have to be taken into her heart, sooner or later.

Mar didn't talk much but he worked hard, and little by little she came to know a good deal about him. She came

[19

to know, for instance, that his mother had been dead ten years; he had been spoiled in some ways, and in others treated with absurd severity by his father who concentrated all his own hopes and fears on this only child. The boy was both old and young for his age; he had learned to respond to the need of affection of the old, had already spent some secret source in himself, was, Hilary sometimes imagined, already gutted by his father's demands, too anxious to meet that measure to be quite himself. She looked for some hardness, for the hard core that might protect him. Now and then she had had intimations that it was there, if one dug down deep enough, but his surfaces were still quivering. He was here, living with his grandfather, because he had gone to pieces in his second year at Amherst, couldn't study, he told Hilary, was "shot to Hell" as he put it, but he didn't tell her why or what had happened, majored in chemistry (his father's idea, no doubt), had done all right for grades, well enough anyway so the college would take him back when he felt ready "to go back to the grind." When he talked about Amherst, and he very rarely did, there was a sort of deadness in his tone, as if he stood before a blank wall. His father had done the right thing out of terror (the alternative was a psychiatrist), had sent Mar to his grandfather for six months, hoping that time itself, and a boat to sail, might mend whatever had been broken. The boat had been old Hemmer's idea; in his view there was nothing the sea couldn't cure. And Hilary approved. The old man let the boy come and go as he pleased; for the first time in his life Mar was free to live alone with himself.

Hilary was soon aware that he had found his way to her door not because he needed the pier, though having it handy saved him a considerable walk, but because he needed a woman around. It took longer for her to realize that there had been something else than a hunger for a feminine atmosphere in the back of his mind, something more definite: he wanted to find out about her as a writer. He was curious about her work. And this despite his almost total ignorance where literature was concerned. But this absence of the predigested and preconceived enhanced his value in Hilary's eyes. She saw that he paid attention to things, that he listened when she explained how to prune an apple tree or why the compost heap was layered as it was, that he handled tools with rare respect, and above all that he was closely observant. She discovered that she cared what he might think about her poems; she was excited when she handed over the piles of books, as if this ignorant boy and his opinion mattered to her more than she was quite willing to admit. How would they look to him? Even now, old, and even at last, famous, she never had handed her work over to anyone without an inner tremor: every flaw leapt out. There seemed to be no single really good poem to show for all the years. But she felt the tremor now because she was handing her work over to someone absolutely open, ignorant of the world, unaware of what "they" had said or had not said, and it had become a test.

There was no gratifying explosion of praise. But while

they worked together, Hilary standing under a tree, Mar high up with the pruning shears, the boy would suddenly say something. He never talked except in some such awkward situation; his voice murmured from a tree or by a stone wall where he was kneeling to weed. "How did you happen to notice that about the lilac buds?" "When you begin a poem what comes first?"

"You know an awful lot about people," he announced one day.

"I've lived a long time."

"You knew a lot when you were young."

"Doesn't one?" she challenged.

But there was no answer. Mar trudged off with a load of dead leaves on the pitchfork, tossed them onto the compost heap, and came back, his shoulders drooping.

"Maybe we had better stop."

"I'm not tired," he sounded cross.

"Then hold up your shoulders. You look like an old man."

"I'm tired inside, not outside."

"Yes," she said matter-of-factly, "I expect you are."

"I'm tired of feeling so much."

"Good God, boy, you've only just begun!" Hilary shouted. She cursed her violence, for he shut up like a clam, didn't speak again that morning, all knotted up. Hilary was aware that he slept badly. Sometimes he turned up for work when he had been out in the boat since four or five o'clock in the morning.

"You're driving yourself."

"Something drives me." Then he had blurted out, "I wish I could write poems."

"It's one way of meeting the enemy."

"What enemy?"

"One's self, of course."

"Yes, I suppose so," he said without enthusiasm.

"Sooner or later you've got to come to terms with whatever it is, Mar."

He had shot her one of his intent looks but had not answered. Hilary had begun to understand how like a wild animal he was; she held her peace. Then he suddenly took a piece of crumpled paper out of his pocket and handed it to her without a word. It was a crude jumble of suffering and self-hatred.

"Yes," Hilary said, handing it back to him. "One of those letters one writes to oneself. As a poem, not anything yet."

"I know."

"Why do you have to hate yourself?" she asked, busying herself with the trowel.

"I can't tell you," he answered after a considerable pause. And that was all that day. Hilary did not know she had such patience in her, but she was learning.

The day came when he asked, "Have you ever—I mean, in all those love poems—are any of them—?" He was red in the face. "I mean, what sort of love are you talking about?" Now it was out, he did not take his eyes off her.

"All kinds, I suppose." What was he getting at, so circuitously and so purposefully?

"Could you tell me just what people you had loved

when you were about my age?"

"Woof!" Hilary took out one of her father's handker-
chiefs and wiped her face and neck. "Too hot! Come and
sit down on the wall, and I'll try to remember."

"You don't *remember!*" Mar flung down his cutters with
a rough angry gesture.

"Well, at least you didn't throw them at me! It was only
a manner of speaking—people slip in and out of one's consciousness, don't you know?"

"Mine don't."

"Oh well, you are obsessed by one person, I expect."
Hilary paid no attention to his reaction whatever it was,
but sat down on the wall and became fascinated by a bee
making its way into the apple blossom close at hand. Mar
watched her.

"To be precise," she uttered at last, "when I was your
age I had been madly in love with a woman a good deal
my senior, with an old man, a doctor, briefly with a nurse
in the hospital, and then of course," she added, as if it
were in some way irrelevant, "with the man I married."

"You can't have loved all those people in the way I
mean," Mar said crossly.

"I loved them in the way one loves at any age—if it's
real at all—obsessively, painfully, with wild exultation;
with guilt, with conflict; I wrote poems to and about them;
I put them into novels (disguised of course); I brooded
upon why they were as they were, so often maddening,
don't you know? I wrote them ridiculous letters. I lived
with their faces. I knew their every gesture by heart. I

stalked them like wild animals. I studied them as if they were maps of the world—and in a way, I suppose they were." She had spoken rapidly, on the defensive . . . if he thought she didn't know what she was talking about! "Love opens the doors into everything, as far as I can see, including and perhaps most of all, the door into one's own secret, and often terrible and frightening, real self."

Mar stamped out his cigarette and retrieved the cutters. "Thanks," he said and made as if to go back to work.

"Come back here, and tell me what eats you!"

He stood about twelve feet away, glaring.

"Utter, man!" But she did not wait for his answer, carried along on her own torrent. "I'm not afraid!"

"Afraid of what?"

"Afraid of feeling, you poop! It's people that matter, Mar, not sexes or ages." Then as suddenly as she had begun, she stopped, gave her light laugh, looked at him quizzically, "I suppose you knew you would open Pandora's box with that question. . . . Who is this fellow?"

It was a guess, but not based on nothing. And Hilary had decided that one of the privileges of old age was that no holds were barred. You were permitted to be absolutely honest. But she knew she had taken a risk. Her absurd heart was beating so fast she felt it pulsing in her throat, as if she were a frog! Would he dash away and never come back?

No, he sat down some distance away, hands between his knees, rocking back and forth.

"You got married!"

It was the last remark Hilary had expected to hear and she was startled into laughter. "Why not? It's not a crime as far as I know." Then she added quite gently, "I consider myself a total human being . . . do you think I'm a monster?"

"No. I think I am." His voice had gone dead. She mustn't lose him now. She mustn't by clumsiness or violence slam the door. How to keep it open? By rambling on, she sensed, give him time.

"So you have got yourself deep into some real feeling, and instead of thanking God that you are not a zombie like most people I see about, you decide you are a monster! Mar," she spoke slowly, testing every word, "it's hard to be growing up in this climate where sex at its most crude and cold is O.K. but feeling is somehow indecent. The monsters are those who go rutting around like monkeys, not those who choose to be human whatever it costs, and it costs a great deal, of course." Mar was silent, but she felt the concentrated attention he was giving her. "The first time you ever came here, I recognized you."

"You did?" he asked, visibly afraid. "What do you mean, 'recognized'?"

"I saw you as a person of primary intensity—they are rare. They live in Hell a good part of their lives, a Hell of their own making, but they are the only people who ever amount to anything, as far as I can see. You've got to accept that it's going to be tough all the way to be the person you are, but do you honestly think one can ever regret loving? The odd thing of course is that we so often choose inappropriate people—I grant you that!" And she laughed her queer light laugh, queer because it sounded so young, and so vulnerable, even shy. "Well," she said as if she were throwing down a glove, "I'll tell you the truth. I loved my husband, but . . . , others touched the poet as he did not. It's mysterious."

"Yes. . . ." Mar uttered only one word, but Hilary knew that she must be very quiet, not let her enormously articulate person overwhelm or break the small thread that was at last there between them, the thread of communion when two human beings, whatever their age or sex may be, give themselves away. It does not happen often; it never happens lightly, and when it has happened, there is a bond between the two that nothing can ever wholly destroy.

"I'm not afraid. It's other people." The story, withheld so long, poured out; Hilary had not been wrong in her guess. The only real friend Mar made at Amherst was a young instructor in chemistry, Rufus Gilbert; they had come to know each other because they shared an interest in birds and soon made a habit of going out at five on Saturday mornings, on long walks in the country.

Of course such friendships do not go unnoticed, and a passion for bird-watching is not quite the regular thing. No doubt the gang at the dormitory had been waiting for a chance to get at Mar, who was something of a maverick anyway, and had a way of vanishing into silence. The more

precious his friendship with Rufus became, the more se-
cretive he was about it, the more the pack instinct was
roused against him. It began with the usual razzing; Mar
was followed by whistles and birdcalls when he crossed
the campus. Once the gang followed the two young men
and cawed like crows from behind some bushes: that time
Rufus had turned on them with such contempt that they
had gone rather sheepishly about their business. But the
barbarians were aroused and out for blood; they egged
each other on, and finally openly jeered at Gilbert in the
class room. This time he was dismayed and upset enough
himself to go to one of the Deans for advice. The Dean
had called Mar in for a friendly talk (oh with the best in-
tentions, no doubt!), but, as Hilary guessed, he had not
known how to go about it at all. Even the fringes of this
subject aroused so much fear, of course, that it was usually mishandled by people in authority, as if they were
not dealing with loyalty and love!

"The filthy bastard made me feel filthy!" Mar shouted.
The tight coil was sprung at last.

"No doubt," Hilary said gently, "he was scared to
death."

"Oh he didn't say anything outright. It was all insinuations. Slimy insinuations."

"And there was no truth in them?"

"Why should I tell you?" Mar shouted at her as if she
were now the enemy herself.

"No reason. Except I want to understand."

Mar leapt to his feet and stood over Hilary in an attitude that she sensed was threatening. Because she felt a threat, she lifted her head and looked up at him, meeting his glance full on. He did not lower his eyes; she could see the pupils widen. He was black in his sacred fury.

"So you can 'help,' I suppose." It was a slap in the face.

"So I can understand. For me, not for you." And she broke the tension by challenging him, "Don't you know me yet as the selfish brute I am?"

"Hard as a diamond." It was good to see this gangling boy take on power. She had not misjudged him.

"In a way, yes," she granted. "Hard as a diamond at the center. How do you suppose one survives, feeling so much (as you would say), if one is not?"

"What makes the diamond?"

"White heat, Mar! What do you think? One has to endure a little more than the jeers of college boys before one is through." Hilary felt stirred up, troubled, fired. Suddenly she wanted to get away to her desk, to write a poem, to be left in peace like a lion bearing off a great chunk of meat. But she had to listen, as Mar spoke out. "I endured more than that," he told her.

Perhaps the hostile atmosphere around him and Rufus had lit the fuse. They met rarely and felt nervous when they did meet, too aware of each other. Finally the delicate web of sensation, nerve, trust, anxiety, and love, stretched so taut between them, had snapped. It was Rufus' suggestion that they go off campus for the weekend in his car.

There in a Motel it had all happened, for Mar the first

intoxicating experience of touch, of discovering inch by inch another body like his own, discovering it with awe, with tenderness, of being able to feel in the marrow of his bones his own sensation touching another in just the same way, above all of finding a climactic outlet at last for all the pent-up flood of feeling he had had to contain for so long. "I was alive!" He shouted in his rage. "I felt no guilt, do you understand?"

"Yes."

"Do you remember what it's like?" he asked in a hard voice.

"Yes."

"I felt holy. I felt I had just been born." Hilary caught the rasp in the hard voice like weeping. "Next morning Rufus wouldn't speak to me. He doesn't answer my letters. He's through."

"It was too much for him," Hilary said quietly, remembering the Dean and knowing very well what it must have been to have a pail of garbage thrown at this shining grace. "He panicked, don't you see?"

"And he's right. And I'm wrong. That's why I go out and sail half the night, don't you *see?*"

Well, it was worse and harder than she had supposed. She got up without a word, picked up the pitchfork, and went back to the iris bed and began to dig out hunks of grass. Mar stood there and watched her. Suddenly she flung down the tool in a gesture reminiscent of his own a few moments before. "Right? Wrong?" she said. "He doesn't hear the mermaids singing, and you do. But that doesn't mean he's right, does it? Or maybe even that what's right for you is right for him, dear boy." She walked over and put a hand on his shoulder in a fraternal gesture. "The trouble is you've got to get through to him inside yourself; you've got to *understand* him, Mar, him as well as yourself . . . tough row to hoe." She stood there with both hands in the pockets of her smock, rocking slightly on her heels. "The only way I can imagine doing it is to write some real poems. Poetry has a way of teaching one what one needs to know . . . if one is honest."

It was as if she and the boy were standing in a great cleared place. As if everything were to be begun again, for her as well as for him. When she told him to write poems, she was addressing her self also. Troubled, moved, she knew in herself the chaos that had to be born somehow out into harmony, had to be clarified. She felt the curious humming in her ears, the pressure.

"Do you think I can? You said the first one was bad."

"It was bad," she flashed back. "You don't learn how in a day. Poetry is not feeling."

"What is it, then?"

"Of course feeling first, but anyone can do that! Making a poem is something else, the ordering, the understanding of feeling. Not being, making." She came to the point abruptly. "Begin by getting this Rufus down . . . a portrait, watching for birds maybe. Oh I don't know. *You* know!" She gave him a keen hard look and decided to take the risk. "That poem was full of self-pity, Mar. You can't afford self-pity. Too much is at stake. Your whole life maybe. Use your bean, start thinking!"

"It seems to me I have been doing nothing else!"

"Going around in a circle isn't thinking. You have to find some way to get outside it, don't you know? Try making a poem as if it were a table, clear and solid, standing there outside you."

"I don't know how," he said frowning his sullen frown.

"Well, there's nothing like trying. You're all slack and seedy, slouching about here. Get your teeth into something hard!"

His eyes narrowed. "You should have been a teacher."

"Oh no," Hilary laughed, "that kind of power doesn't interest me." Then she took a cigarette out of her pocket and lit it, blowing out the smoke with a kind of joy. "Besides if you teach, you have to take them as they come, the dull, the amorphous, the half-baked. You have to care. I'm too busy with my own problems."

"*I'm* half-baked. You just told me so."

"Well, at least you're in the oven!" On that they fell into a gust of giggles, and felt easy with each other again. It was the beginning of their real relationship, as if the decks were cleared. Mar knew now that she could accept him as he was; he could go to the limit of his being with her and not be denied. She accepted his suffering and his love as realities. For Hilary there was a listening ear again, a tension set up: as he began to fumble his way toward poetry, she felt in some way challenged by him, herself, as a poet. As if he were some jinni released from a bottle, he made huge strides, came into a kind of power so quickly that sometimes Hilary felt a stab of envy. She had the wit to lend him her Encyclopedia of Mythology, and somehow or other the tales of the great amoral beasts and gods unlocked his imagination. The poems were rough, violent, and rather gory, but they had thrust, and he was finding a style of his own, a short-cut language, often ungrammatical. He had an eye for the shape of a poem on the page. He used abrupt rhythms and . . . , a good sign, Hilary felt . . . he fought her criticisms with asperity, showed all the arrogance of the person who knows what he is doing. They often got angry with each other. For Mar took his turn at criticizing; the roughness, the honesty was tonic. Hilary cut her own poems to the bone, found herself drawing on the masculine side of her talent as she had not done since . . . really not since she had been a young girl. It was salutary to pit the new poems against someone so young and intransigeant—so ignorant too—who would have none of her hardwon virtuosity, who forced her back and back to the essence, who brought out the crude, original person. They fought bitterly, sometimes over a single word. Often she was in a rage when he left, but the rage shot adrenalin through her, gave her the strength to begin a poem again, tear it apart, make it harder and stronger so she could hurl it at Mar the next day in triumph. She had not imagined that she would be so fertilized by a human being again.

Nevertheless, she thought, as she did finally get out of bed to begin the morning chores, she could have done without his violence and his depression just today. What she needed today was not the romantic impulse but the classic consideration. She needed distance, order, and not to be troubled by someone else's problems. What could be the matter? Drat the boy! She had better pull on some clothes. It was nearly eight.

The phone rang as she was carrying the tray downstairs, always a perilous business because she couldn't see her feet. The imperative ring hit her like a bullet. She stood halfway down while a wave of dizziness seized her and only just managed to get there before the ringing stopped.

"Oh Alice. . . . I'm all right, just out of breath . . . , no, not possibly . . . , my dear woman, I never go to cocktail parties. Masses of people make me feel ill. . . . No doubt I am a lion, but I will not roar at your party! I sound cross? I am cross. What I want is to see you in peace, don't you see? Not to have to get all gigged up and behave myself! . . . Well, sorry."

She put the receiver down, furious at her own agitation. Guilt would be sure to follow; it would take an hour for her to convince herself that if old friends tried to use her, now that she was suddenly a social asset again, they might as well learn. Oh dear. If one allowed a single crack in one's armor, the wounds began to ache. She had not called on old Mrs. Balch for weeks, and she had promised to go and read Rose Macaulay's letters aloud to her, and poor Philip was waiting, she knew, to be asked down over night for "a good talk" as he put it, which meant endless complaints about himself, his health, his loneliness, the general stupidity of the world, etc. I get so tired, she said to herself, resuming the dialogue, if they only knew. "They" who said, "How wonderful it must be to be a writer," as if writing were a game of solitaire and one did not have to fight like a tiger for a moment's peace and quiet! Not to mention the struggle itself, the daunting of the doddering old servant, the persistent will necessary to get down to it when one had finally clawed one's way through to a piece of time.

Well, she was dressed anyway, in one of the artist's smocks she had used to wear in Paris—Mar liked them, and he would turn up, she supposed, any minute now. She paused for a moment at the mirror on the kitchen wall to be reassured. "Pale as death," she uttered to the mirror. The night had taken its toll. You can't review a whole life, a life like mine, in twelve hours, and not feel the weight. "Up and at 'em!" she said aloud.

First, the dishes must be washed. Fortunately she had had a window cut over the sink, so washing the dishes could be done absent-mindedly while looking out for birds. That oriole she had heard might be in the apple tree; also she could keep an eye out for Mar coming across the wall.

But the dishes were dried and put away, and neither the oriole nor Mar had deigned to make an appearance. Hilary then made a list of things to do—she hoped she would be able to decipher it later on. It said "anchovy sandwiches for tea." It said, "Be sure the tea pot is polished. Refill the sugar bowl. Lay the fire. Dig up an earthworm for the turtles if time. . . ." Her peace of mind was dependent on lists, but lately her hand had become so illegible that sometimes "house" looked like "mouse," and she had hilarious moments when she read "Clean the mouse" or "prepare for marriage," which she finally realized was actually "prepare the garbage" (the garbage collector came once a week).

She gave one more anxious glance outdoors. No Mar. Well then, nothing to do but keep going. First things first, and the first thing was to take a look at the living room and see to the flowers. "They" always said, "What beautiful flowers you have!" But "they" never imagined how much time this irrelevant passion took from her work, at least an hour every morning in summer. No man would trouble about such things; the imaginary man in her mind got up at six, never made his bed, did not care a hoot if there were a flower or not, and was at his desk as bright as a button, at dawn, with a whole clear day before him while some woman out of sight was making a delicious hot stew for his supper. Hilary had often asked herself why she felt the need for flowers . . . , but there it was. The house felt empty and desolate without them. They were silent guests who must be made happy, and who gave the atmosphere a kind of soul. She went out with her scissors and cut two or three daffodils, one white one and one or two yellow ones, and a few poeticus narcissi, and let them arrange themselves in a Venetian glass, taking it with her into the big room, standing there in the doorway, seeing it all through the eyes of the interviewers, New York eyes, sophisticated eyes. Would they feel the order and the

peace, as much a creation as any poem she had written?
This room, too, gathered together a huge complex of living
and harmonized it, all focused on the small intimate
glimpse of sea cut through the scrub and brush, framed in
French windows at the end. But would they disdain the
flowered chintz on the sofa as old-fashioned? Would they
register the two Impressionist paintings as not quite first
class?

Hilary went to the Venetian mirror, set the flowers
on the table under it, then walked back to stand at the fireplace and observe the effect. There in the mirror across the
room she caught a glimpse of herself as Sargent had cap-
tured her, in the drawing over the mantel, at twenty five.
There stood Age with Youth, like a ghost, suspended over
her head. Without her glasses, Hilary saw the two figures
as slightly blurred, as if seen through water . . . , they
seemed strangely alike, as perhaps they were; one does not
become less oneself with the years, but more so; that
self-intoxicated, quizzical young charmer was less than
the Hilary confronting her with just the same slightly
mocking lift of her chin.

She was not really seeing with her eyes. As always in
this room, she was borne away on half-conscious stretches
of memory. What "they" never understood about her soli-
tary life was that it was a solitude so inhabited by the past,
that she was never alone in it, except sometimes in the rich
disorder of her work room upstairs. There the past did not
exist; it was all and only the arduous joyful present.

The Venetian mirror, eighteenth century, in a delicate

scrolled gold frame, the glass clouded as if a ghostly breath had clouded it, had been a wedding present, the only thing Hilary had managed to keep with her from that time. It had hung in hotel rooms, in lodgings, in rented cottages in England, in Vermont, who knows where? For Hilary it kept the natural warmth of her marriage alive, far better than did the faded photographs of herself and Adrian in ridiculous dated clothes. So now what came vividly to her mind, with its particular appropriateness to the day, was the morning when she and Adrian had first hung the mirror in their Chelsea flat. She remembered a beam of sunlight crossing its watery depths, and Adrian saying,

"There, now we can invite a duchess to tea!"

Hilary had always longed for someone who would tease her, and love her, and accept her as she was. She could lie in the crook of Adrian's arm and stare at the ceiling, and feel absolutely sheltered and safe. He was as limpid as a Mozart Sonata, as unassuming and deep. When she had tantrums, he just looked at her with delight, told her how pretty she looked when she was angry, and hauled her out to walk it off along the river, taking her whole arm and holding it close to his side, so clearly confident of his own power, that she believed it, believed that he was the answer to all doubt, that she was moored at last. It was immensely real on the level on which it existed, their marriage, rooted in the endearing physical world—riding (Adrian had taught her to jump, and how patient and gentle he was when she panicked!), dancing, laughing, making love. Those three precious years had been like a

long summer holiday, a rest, the only one she would ever
have, from obsession, anxiety, and work. Once Adrian had
found her sitting at the little chinoiserie desk (it had no
resemblance to a work table), her chin on her hand, and
had asked,

"A penny for your thoughts!"

"They're not worth a penny," she had said, because she
could not bear to hurt him, and because also she wanted to
pretend even to herself that her life with him was all she
needed or wanted. How could she say to this total being,
"I am still sometimes haunted by demons. I want to write
poems. I want to feel the pull of the impossible again. . . .
I want to be myself."

"Aren't you yourself with me?" he would have asked,
smiling in the pleasure of himself, in the pleasure of her,
his wife. He would have asserted their union by lifting her
right off her chair and taking her to bed where the particu-
lars of selfhood were submerged in the great primal darkness, where their union was deep and complete enough to
transcend the personal, and Hilary felt carried out of herself on a tide of urgency and renewal. Why then did she
sometimes wake the next morning with depression hang-
ing over her like a fog? Would it have been different if
they had created the child they each wanted so much? It
was troubling to feel sometimes so empty, emptied out of
herself.

Adrian, on the other hand, was driven by an inexhausti-
ble urge for life, and life for him meant using his physical
being to the limit of his strength, and beyond. He refused

to pay any attention to his old wounds (shrapnel had had to be extracted from four different places), though he sometimes felt sick after riding too hard, but laughed it off, took some medicine, and a half an hour later was off to play tennis. After all, he had survived the trenches. What could touch him now? And if he took to drinking rather a lot, so did everyone else in their world. They were surrounded by ghosts; all of them like Adrian had lost all but two or three of the friends they had known at Eton and Oxford. The gay parties, where women always outnumbered men, had their poignance. You could be wild, funny, eccentric, but you must not weep or ever, ever look back; war was the one taboo subject, but it was always there at the feast, looking out of a drunken eye, or making a loud laugh suddenly harsh and bitter.

Sometimes lying in the dark, hearing Adrian's heart beat against her temple as she lay in the crook of his arm, Hilary felt his mystery, the mystery of all those who had come back and could not talk about it. Somewhere inside that warm, life-giving body, there was a great black cavern; there was more death than could be stomached. She ran a finger along his cheek, and down his neck, and across his great shield of a breast, touched the bone under her palm, and came to the crisscross thread of the wound, as if she were exploring a sacred object; she felt reverence, but no real understanding. What could their life be like as it went on? What are we rooted in? she wondered in those panics of early dawn. Adrian's job was a made job in an insurance company of which an uncle was member of the board. It meant little or nothing except as a painless way of paying bills until he came into his inheritance. She, on the other hand, was famous or infamous as the writer of a first novel which had had a succès de scandale . . . the last thing she had wanted or expected, not realizing that honest probing of matters generally discussed with lifted eyebrows at dinner tables could shock. And, in fact, her marriage had proved a refuge from anonymous letters and a kind of notoriety which induced such distaste in its subject that Hilary thought for a time that she would never again commit herself to print. She married Adrian in a total revulsion from one part of herself, yet whether she ever published a word again or not she could not stop being the person she was. There was the rub! She was young, witty, on the defensive, and more than once at a dinner party, she had let herself go, had talked from her own center, honestly, had enjoyed feeling her powers in action, until she had caught Adrian's look across the table, a troubled look, a slightly hostile look. Afterwards she had an attack of self-doubt. "I talked too much, didn't I?" she asked while they drank cocoa before going to bed.

"You were brilliant."

"Oh."

"What's wrong?"

"It's evidently wrong to be brilliant. You didn't like it, did you?"

"Well," Adrian said warily, for by now he had learned to be wary, "You are rather intense, you know. You take everything so hard, Hilary . . . it isn't quite. . . ."

"Done?" And she could hear the rising shrillness in her voice, feel the tiger she tried so hard to keep out of sight, begin to pace and lash its tail. "Sometimes I feel I can never be my real self here. I'm an American, after all."

"Yes, darling, I know," he said gently. "But could you be your real self at home, if by that you mean being more naked and more honest than most people ever dare to be?"

The tiger began to pace up and down, rather incongruous in her short, low-waisted evening dress, with a cup of cocoa in one hand and a cigarette in the other.

"Hilary, please don't!"

"Don't what?"

"Don't pace about as if you were caged."

"I am caged! I don't fit in, and I never will. You are so right. It's not being American—it's being myself. I'm a writer, Adrian!"

"Well, what if you are? You're a *succès fou.*"

"I hate that book!"

"Then write another you like better," he said rather crossly.

"I want a baby, not a book!" She silenced him, but it was an evasion, and she knew it. She had surreptitiously been making notes for a new novel, but what she had in mind was ironic, and it would surely hurt Adrian. She *was* caged, caged by being in love with, and married to, a man whose life pattern seemed to her both trivial and confining. She was caged also by the demands of housekeeping, by the late hours they kept, so she never woke up really fresh with the extra psychic energy at her command necessary for writing a single sentence. Housekeeping terrified and absorbed her, and she felt challenged to a kind of perfectionism which gave her no leeway as far as time went. In this mood of emptiness and frustration, she went down to Kent alone to spend a weekend with Adrian's parents. Whatever ambivalence Hilary might experience in her relation to the society in which she found herself, her response to the cherished, tender, rich countryside was absolute. Her love of the shaped, the orderly (she had never wholly responded to the unpruned, thick, second growth of New England) could bask in this landscape created slowly over the centuries until it had now a kind of perfection. It made her feel drunk with pleasure to walk, as she did that weekend, with Adrian's mother, through great open groves of trees, across patches of bluebells that sometimes in certain lights gave the illusion of water, so blue and thick they were. To Hilary it seemed a kind of magic not to have to struggle through underbrush as one so often did in New England—it was like certain wonderful dreams where one did not walk so much as float a few inches above the ground.

"Heaven!" she murmured.

She had sensed in Margaret Stevens from the beginning the same passionate response. She, who was in every other way so reserved, so delicately poised, became a different person out of doors, as if she shed a skin when she knelt by a border in one of those big straw hats tied under her chin with a chiffon scarf, and weeded fiercely. Now she walked with long free strides beside her daughter-in-law.

"Isn't it amazing that one never remembers what spring will be? I had forgotten about the beech leaves—"

"You must come down more often, Hilary."

"Adrian wants to, but we get so involved in parties and things."

They walked companionably along while that last sentence hung in the air between them. Margaret Stevens was an exceedingly shy person who hid her shyness under perfect manners, and wore it with grace, partly because she was such a delightfully pretty woman; she had Adrian's clear blue eyes, but just a shade darker and a shade more gentle; she always smelled of lavender and refused to follow the fashion for short frocks, so now Hilary thought she looked just right in a plain rather long blue linen skirt, and a frilly white blouse under a soft pink sweater. (With what extraordinary vividness the scene came back to her, even to the sunlight catching in the diamond on Margaret Stevens' delicate brown hand.) Finally she had spoken.

"I'm a little anxious about Adrian . . . are you?" She instinctively included Hilary, not to seem critical. "I do rather dislike this fashion of so many cocktails. It seems a little . . . a little out of character. Or am I being outrageously old-fashioned?" And she gave Hilary one of her dazzling smiles, meant to dazzle, and so, to hide in, Hilary guessed.

"We're dancing on the graves, and no one really forgets it ever. So Adrian drinks too much—we all do."

"Does he enjoy his work?"

"He never talks about it." One is not a daughter-in-law

for nothing, Hilary thought, as the magic ease of the morning began to flow away and she must make the effort to be again her married self, not her *self*.

"You are very much in love." Was it a question? A judgment? What was it?

"Yes, we are."

"And you are very different." Hilary waited for what would come next. What did come next was not at all what she had expected. "I suppose you are hard at work yourself on another book?"

"I make notes. There never seems to be any real time . . . , and I'm so awkward, such a novice about running the flat still. Maybe writing is irrelevant really. . . ."

"Oh no!" The response was immediate and firm. "Your writing must be for you what horses are for Adrian," and she laughed. "It does sound a bit odd, but you must feel only really and fully alive when you are doing it, as Adrian does when he is hunting."

"Yes," Hilary answered, feeling like a starving person who has just been given a piece of bread, "Yes, it is like that. It's monstrous, but nothing seems real to me unless I can say it. This morning, for instance, this walk, all the time I am trying to find a word for that green of the beech leaves. Why not just *see* them? It's idiotic!"

"Women are so much more conscious than men . . . , even when they are not writers, you know."

"Do you think so? Really?"

"Conscious or self-conscious," and again she laughed, as if to soften perspicacity behind the screen of the feminine.

It was what women were supposed to do, and what Hilary found so hard to do herself.

"What I really want is to write poems," Hilary uttered on the wave of intimacy. She would never have admitted this to Adrian. She felt, perhaps wrongly, that he would have been terrified; that it would erect a barrier between them, as if an old friend had announced that he was taking Holy Orders.

"Oh, I'm happy about that," Margaret said, bending down to look a wood anemone in the face, lifting it on its stalk. "I think perhaps you are on the right track. Perhaps the novel was not your thing, really. Brilliant as it was."

It is always hard to hear the buried truth from another person, and Hilary did not answer.

"I'm being outrageously frank with you." Hilary felt a gentle hand on her shoulder. "I hope you take it as a compliment. But you are such an honest person yourself. And that is a responsibility."

"Yes," Hilary uttered, full of pain. "It is."

"Why did you fall in love with Adrian, I wonder? You know so much more than he does . . . believe me, dear Hilary, I am grateful, grateful that you did."

They walked on in silence while Hilary wrestled with her answer. Could she be honest now? Could she take the risk?

"You are right about the novel. I didn't know what I was doing. I am dismayed by the success it has had. Don't you see, Adrian appeared in the middle of all that brouhaha. He seemed like good bread after too much champagne.

Margaret . . . ," it was the first time Hilary had called her mother-in-law by her first name. "It is hard to be a woman and a writer. Lately I have begun to think it impossible. I want to feel sane and whole. I want what Adrian is, that absolute entity. The safety of it, the peace." But she couldn't leave it at that. It sounded so smug. "It seems fantastic that such a person can love me. It seems like a miracle. It is a miracle."

"Adrian is my son," Margaret said. "I want him to be happy. He has married out of his sphere, someone with a touch of genius. . . . I have grown fond of you, Hilary. I want you two to be happy. But life with Adrian. . . ." She paused and gave Hilary a quizzical look, "Life with Adrian is going to ask all your tenderness, all your womanliness. . . ."

"I know," Hilary breathed. "He's an angel."

"Hardly!" Margaret was quick to detect a false note. They exchanged a look of amusement, a look in which Hilary admitted that she had been caught out.

"Oh well," she amended, laughing, "not an angel maybe, but an angel compared to me!"

"It is a somewhat irritating thing about men that they are so often good . . . good because they don't know the half of it, or because," and Margaret smiled her delicious dazzling smile, "they only know the half of it."

"How do you know so much?"

"I settled for being a woman. I wonder whether you can," and quickly she went on, as if to cover or put a dressing on a wound. "I have been blessed with a husband who, if I was unhappy, never knew it, and if he had known it would not have understood why." She added, "There are enormous comforts in the kind of life I lead."

"Such as the garden?"

"Such as the garden . . . ," and Margaret left it at that.

"What are you really asking of me?" Hilary stopped and lifted her head to the great beeches not thinking it odd that, having asked the crucial question, she was also saying over a series of adjectives which might possibly define that particular translucent green over head.

"I can't ask you to be less than yourself. But I do wish your life were a little less hectic, Hilary, for Adrian's sake as well as yours. His job, I quite see, isn't a real root. But your poems, if you could settle in to write them—your poems might be a kind of root—women seem to be stronger than men, these days."

"The men have been mortally wounded," Hilary said. "Yes."

And Hilary had tried, for Margaret's sake, as well as for her own. But it was very queer. She was sometimes moved to tears just seeing Adrian walk into the room, like some hero without a purpose, smiling his great warm smile, but what ever she felt for him, it had nothing to do with writing poetry.

Standing there looking at her two selves reflected in the Venetian mirror, Hilary wondered what would have become of them if Adrian had not died. . . . Would the tiger in her finally have turned to rend? The starved, growing, fierce tiger of the imagination who was unappeased?

As it was, Adrian had died his own death, wrapped in his own kind of violence, falling over a jump and breaking his neck. It was so sudden, so final, that Hilary went to pieces; she cried a great deal, aware that this also was something "not done"; and she cried perhaps not so much out of grief, as out of some indefinable sense of being now cut off from everything, and most of all from herself. She had a wild hope for a month that she might be pregnant, but that hope proved false. She knew then that never again in her life would she find comfort, the perfect simple comfort of being held in the arms of Adrian. That phase of her life was over for good. So intense was her feeling about it that one day in Kent when she saw the old cat lying stretched out in the sun, perfectly relaxed, she burst into tears and rushed out of the room. Why? It had become in an instant the image of deprivation. But she could not explain this even to herself, only accept Margaret's tender care, accept the trays that found their way to her room, sometimes with a single rose in a little glass by her cup, or a book of poems. They had hovered on the verge of intimacy for those weeks, but the thread of communication between them depended too much on someone who was not there, of whom Margaret could not speak. Hilary fled as soon as she decently could, got herself a job in London in a publishing house, and began to try to come to terms with her tiger. How cruel memory is, forgetful memory that drops whole lives out without a qualm! It occurred to her, standing in the brilliant morning light, forty years later—and surrounded by her own life, her life alone—

[49

that among the letters she had unbundled last night, there had been a touching one from Adrian's father, the ink almost faded, thanking her for having given Adrian "those brief years of happiness." Tears sprang to her eyes, because she could not remember the old man's face. . . .

Hilary wished she could stop the shuttle which for the last week had been so inexorably weaving the past and the present together. . . . She walked quickly down the big room to the French windows. No Mar. Perhaps after all he had been put off by her nervousness. But he shouldn't make me so anxious, she thought, it's not fair! And on an impulse, simply to get back firmly into the present, she went to the telephone and called Mary back.

"It's me, Hilary. I'm sorry I was cross, Mary, but I feel so badgered these days! Besides, you know very well I am not fit for society. I get overexcited and say the wrong thing. . . . You know, I do! . . . Besides, this afternoon two young people are coming to interview me about my whole *oeuvre*. . . . That's what they said, *oeuvre*. . . . I feel like a hen who has laid a monstrous number of eggs or something. Don't laugh, I'm serious. . . . Terrified. . . . I've been reading old letters and things to try to get some perspective, a frightful mistake. It has made me dreadfully depressed and confused. . . . Of course it's flattering—of course I shall enjoy it! You are so literal, darling . . . , well—as long as you still love me. . . . Goodbye!"

Sirenica had come to wrap herself around Hilary's legs, rubbing her nose against Hilary's sneakers with passion, and purring ecstatically. But when Hilary bent down to scratch behind the delicate white ears, the cat dashed off, holding her tail high. Wyatt's poem welled up out of this little scene and Hilary was borne out into the garden on the wave of joy, as she found she could recite it still by heart—at least one thing memory had yielded up for keeps.

> *They flee from me that sometime did me seek,*
> *With naked foot stalking within my chamber:*
> *Once I have seen them gentle, tame, and meek,*
> *That now are wild, and do not once remember*
> *That sometime they have put themselves in danger*
> *To take bread at my hand; and now they range,*
> *Busily seeking in continual change.*

"And that's for you, my pussy," Hilary said, as Sirenica leapt into the air, paws outstretched, but missed the butterfly she was after, pretended it was all a gambol, and sat down decorously, tucking her paws in, under a rose bush.

Hilary whistled a self-made tune as she went to the woodshed and got out her basket of gardening tools. On her way back, she heard the oriole give its piercing four notes from somewhere among the apple trees, and dropped the basket to climb swiftly over the stone wall, hoping to catch a glimpse of that orange flame. Elusive bird! Hilary leaned back under each tree, but no luck. She stood quite still and listened, the perplexities and anxieties of the morning gone, as if she had been released from a spell and

[51

allowed back into the world of Now. Even Mar was forgotten, while she noted, as she slowly returned, that the
rose, Nevada, needed spraying, and she simply must weed
the small border along the wall, or it would become a
jungle.

"After all, Sirenica, we have the whole morning. No
work today. . . ."

Any day when Hilary did not sit at her desk was auto-
matically a holiday, even if there were interviewers lying
in wait at the end of it. Soon her fingers were deftly pulling out tufts of grass and violets from around the bleeding
heart; nothing like weeding to unknot the mind, nothing
except the same thing in another sphere, pruning the fat
out of a poem, cutting, shaping, give it space to breathe
in.

"Ow!" Her fingers had struck a rock. Gardening in New
England has its peculiar frustrations, she thought. But
there the rock was, and it must be dug out. She sat down
in the grass to spare her back, but as usual, the rock turned
out to be a lot bigger than she had imagined when she
bruised a finger against one corner of it. It would be a fine
thing if Mar did turn up now to haul it out for her with the
crowbar. Hilary looked hopefully around. Not a sign of
the rascal! "Very well then," she said, and began to scratch
around it with her trowel; it would have been wise to go
and fetch the crowbar herself, but difficulty roused passion;
she was too impatient to make that effort. Instead, she
hauled away with her two hands, pitting her whole
strength against one stone as if her life depended on the

outcome. Finally it gave, sucked out like some huge tooth. Hilary sat back, and felt for the cigarettes in her pocket. But the first puff induced an alarming sensation in her head, as if all the juice were being drawn away, and dizziness set in. "It's such a nuisance," said young Hilary to old Hilary. But old Hilary was frightened, frightened of death. "Lie down, you fool," said old Hilary, and for once she was obeyed. "You can't die yet, you've got too much to do," said young Hilary. And in the center of the vertigo, she experienced the thrust of expectancy and of hope. All the living, all the caring, all the anxiety had only been a prelude to that not impossible poem, the thing that would justify it all, and stop forever the whirling of the past with all its images, make the whole world stand still!

Lying there, waiting, still unable to focus, she threw the cigarette into the grass with a gesture of impatience. She wanted now above all to get to her desk—to see if she could quietly, by stealth, pounce on the final stanza of a poem which had been nagging at her to get itself finished for almost a year; she had unearthed it again the day before while hunting for something else. Oh dear . . . but impatient young Hilary waited. It would not do to try to heave her ancient twin upright, only to have her keel over.

At least when she opened her eyes now, the awful rushing blurr had gone. She looked straight up into apple blossom and noticed a robin's nest she had not known was there. As always after one of these bouts, the sweetness of life flowed back in, so that she would have liked to thank someone, to pray. The bliss of solitude, when it did not

matter a hoot if one lay down on the grass like an old donkey, having been ridiculous enough to strain one's heart!

But where is Mar? She sat bolt upright in the deafening
silence. Would there ever come a time when one was
not waiting for *someone*?

Hilary shivered. A cloud had gone over the sun. Mar
was not the sort to do himself violence, but anxiety could
not be stilled, for human life was always, it seemed, in
peril. Lately the boy had appeared to be so much better,
but she realized that she had been troubled by the look on
his face early that morning; and it haunted her now in her
state of depletion. He had looked ravaged, but in an unattractive way, dissipation rather than grief, shame. What
was it she had read in that brief glimpse before he turned
and ran?

She got up and went indoors, driven by the cold and
anxiety to her desk, the one place where, during the hours
she sat there, neither death nor taxes nor any present trouble could come near. Her desk was set perpendicular to a
dormer window; so she sat with the sea on her left, and on
her right a solid wall of books. Files of all shapes and sizes
were scattered about; she used one as added desk space.
On this, she noted with dismay, was a sheaf of old letters,
part of her last night's orgy. Stupid of her to have left
them there, like wide open eyes she did not want to meet.
Her life, which only a few moments before, had swung
safely in the divine present of the May morning, now
threatened to overpower her. She had come upstairs to
work, not to relive what had better be left like the compost

heap, to its own slow burning and self-renewal.

What had been so disturbing during the night had been to endure the wake of the great wave of memories on which she had been transported, opening up all those boxes . . . the appalling complex of people who had entered deeply into her life, who had influenced, and changed, and enriched her. And it was absolutely untrue, she had discovered, to believe that age would diminish her power both to attract and to be attracted, to rush in to the collision with a new consciousness, to feel herself opening up like a sea anemone in the rich flood of feeling for a new person. Old, young, male, female—her capacity to be touched, to be involved, to *care* was, she realized, that still of a young girl. How did one keep growing otherwise? What was life all about otherwise? What separates us from animals except just this—that we can be moved by each other, and not primarily for sexual purposes? Granted, of course, that any deep collision, any relationship which profoundly affects one comes from the whole person, and can almost instantaneously shift from one phase to another, so that sex is never wholly absent and may come into play. Yes, that was the rub . . . , for then there is conflict. Someone gets hurt. And it was no use remembering that often she had been the hurt one: the fact remained that she had inevitably hurt others. "But I regret nothing," she said aloud and firmly. For it hurts to be alive, and that's a fact, but who can regret being alive and being for others, life-enhancing? We shall be dead a long time. Quite deliberately Hilary stuffed the letters into a

[55

drawer and bent her head toward the much-crossed-out worksheet of the poem she thought she might just possibly take by surprise and bring to an end on this morning of superior tension.

After a time, and when she had murmured some lines aloud, she shot a sheet of paper onto the typewriter and tapped out with one finger what she had in her mind, tore it out, and began to scribble changes and queries into the margins. She became wholly absorbed, was not aware of the crick in her shoulder, nor of the French clock chiming eleven and then twelve. At twelve she laid the sheets aside. It had been a wild hope that she could solve the puzzle in two hours. Still, she had made a start. There was now one really good line, an armature for the whole poem. . . . Yes.

"Good Heavens! The mail!" For once, because she was orbiting outside her usual routine, she had forgotten this daily blessing and curse. Usually she was standing at the mailbox when the postman drove up. Sometimes Mr. Willoughby was the only human being she spoke to during a whole day, and sometimes he brought a piece of fish with him for Sirenica, the shameless flirt, who had laid a spell on him with her blue eyes. But today of course he had long since come and gone; Sirenica was sitting beside the mailbox washing her face. Hilary reached in and found the usual packet of journals and letters. The very sight of it exhausted her, yet there was (she could not deny) always the same stab of expectation and of hope. . . . What surprise, what unexpected joy might be lurking among all the bills and requests for attention? And of course there was *The New York Times*.

As always, when Hilary came out from the burrow of her work room, she saw everything with a rinsed eye. Now she sat down in the rocker in the kitchen and was dazzled by the beauty of a long slanting slab of sunlight on the white plaster wall. One might, she supposed, sit and take it in for half an hour, but say it? Next to impossible. These moments of vision when quite simple things became extraordinary were what she always meant to "get down," but the impulse wavered, or got pushed aside. Hilary had always imagined that one of the blessings of old age would be that one might live by and for these essentials . . . the light on a wall. Instead one dragged around this great complex hive of sensation and feeling. "Bother!" she uttered, eagerly unfolding the *Times* to the obituaries.

Well, thank goodness, for once no one had died. Lately it had been a holocaust—everyone, it seemed, was dying. And what really was the point of living on, if one was to be the sole survivor of one's world? No one to depend on any more, no one who really *mattered*. Hilary could not get accustomed to having become herself the older generation, nor could she really believe that the young might wait for a word of praise from her, as she had waited—so long, always—for a word of praise from her elders. These were dangerous thoughts; she warded off the tide of depression which might begin to rise at any moment now, by turning to the letters. First she tore open several second-class envelopes. Bishops in South Africa asking alms, the

Civil Liberties Union, Core, Care. God knows, they all seemed to think that if you gave your mite, it should be doubled within the month! After this freight of anguish, and the inevitable rousing of guilt and shame— Why was she not richer? Why was she so selfish?—Hilary turned over a long envelope which might prove interesting. It contained a letter from a ninth-grade girl in a school in New Jersey, asking her to say in a few words why she, Hilary, wrote poetry and just how she wrote a poem. Only that! At once Hilary began inventing an answer: Dear Miss So-and-So, You are monstrously lazy and ill-bred; you think nothing of asking me to spend a morning answering two idiotic portmanteau questions.

But of course she would never write any such letter . . . , instead, the effort of toning down her irritation and finding two or three appropriate sentences, might take a half hour tomorrow morning. Bother! It was to be that kind of mail, was it? For the next envelope contained a sheaf of terrible poems with a request for criticism; the hand was elderly; the need, obvious. The third letter she opened, by now exasperated, was from a publisher, asking her to read and, if possible, say a few words about a new novel (on its way in bound galleys under separate cover). There were two more of the same ilk. The house, Hilary sometimes imagined, would be buried under the avalanche of books, and she would never again be able to choose what she would read.

So this was fame at last! Nothing but a vast debt to be paid to the world in energy, in blood, in time. And lucky she who had escaped it for forty-five years!

At last Hilary turned up two personal letters from the huge pile, and tore into them happily. One was from her old school-friend, Nancy, the only one with whom she still kept in touch. Nancy, desperate as usual, though she was now a grandmother, fighting her life out inch by inch, valiant, original. "Dear Nancy!" Hilary murmured as she read, "Oh Hilary didn't you think one would feel less naked in old age? Or at least not quite so desperate? Bob's little boy has leukemia; my own Bob is in one of his remote states when I feel I married a zombie forty years ago. The garden is devoured by slugs. How are you? I hope you are thriving . . . do I really? No, I really hope you are so badgered by having become a celebrity that you will fly over and stay for weeks. You must admit that if we don't manage to meet soon, one of us will be dead and the other, sorry."

No one is happy, Hilary thought, not Mar, not Nancy —and fifty years between them. Am I happy? She asked herself and was surprised to find that the immediate response from some inner part of her being was, "Yes . . . yes and no . . . ," but she did not stop to finish this thought, as she was now immersed in the second personal letter, written in a childish hand from a village in Maine. It was the quarterly report from dear old Susan who had nursed Hilary's mother through her final illness; it was the acknowledgment of the usual check. "Your mother loved the lilacs and now they are in bud, I think of her every day. I never did thank you—or did I?—for the February check. I am getting old and forgetful and you must forgive me. My old cat, Tomboy, died. I thought you would like to know. I buried him under the apple tree. The place seems lonely now. When will you come and see us? I should have said me. Now Tomboy is dead, it is only me."

Dear old Susan. "I shall have to go, of course," Hilary thought. "It is the least I can do." But had her mother loved lilacs?

The sun had gone under a cloud, and that vivid slanting white light was diffused on the wall. My mother, Hilary thought. . . . Did she love the lilacs? How little I knew her, really. Desolation ran through her like an electric current turned on . . . , but I simply must rest, Hilary said to the current, making an effort to turn it off. I must go and lie down. I must shut this out because the interviewers are coming, and I cannot disintegrate. I must meet them, fully armed.

Quickly she made herself a peanut butter sandwich, set it on a tray with a glass of milk, and fled to her bedroom. She pulled the curtains, lay down in the aqueous light, and fell half asleep in a kind of doze, forgetting to eat. It was the mail, of course. It took at least an hour of the day before the reverberations brought in by the mail died down. Foreign matter quite literally broke into one's composure and shattered it with great booming sounds. . . .

Had her mother loved the lilacs? Why had not Hilary ever known this as precisely as did an old nurse, no connection at all, a stranger? Her mother lived on in Susan's awareness as a different person from the one who troubled

Hilary's sleep so often these days. In Susan's hands her mother had become a loving infant . . . all the tenderness locked back through all the years had flowed out to this stranger; Hilary was the outsider, allowed in for brief formal visits. Oh, it was too painful! She turned over, hoping that a different physical position would somehow change the psychic position, but it was no use. "Absurd old woman," young Hilary admonished old Hilary, "pull yourself together. Sit up, drink your milk, and eat your sandwich!"

"Hilary has a fine mind, but she is too emotional," she could hear her mother saying to her father; and during her childhood both her parents devised ways of teaching her what they considered proper control of the indecent extravagence of those wild tears, so often tears of rage. Well, she had learned something: it was to set herself a problem to solve when she was seized by "woe" as Nancy called it. So let's have it out, she admonished herself. *Think* about your mother, old fool, and stop feeling so much; stop weeping over what is irrevocable and finished.

"Irrevocable, maybe," old Hilary answered at once, "but not finished! We may come into the world naked, but we go out of it clothed in anguish."

Where then did it all begin? Her mother and father had been second cousins, members of a vast Boston clan who congregated every summer in Sorrento, Maine, and regarded anyone not born in Boston as deprived and to be treated with faintly condescending kindness; just in the way they regarded anyone who spent money freely as slightly feeble-minded, a person to be spoken of as "Poor David has just bought a yacht," or "those pathetic Richardsons have moved again into—of all things!—a French château on the Maine coast." Their own lives were unassailable in their circumspection, hidden generosity, and good taste. Of course her father had spent a fortune on French Impressionists; no doubt his cousins at that time spoke of him as "Poor Jason . . . , crazy about those French painters," but the joke was on them when their own safe shares in Kruger proved a total loss and Jason's madness a gilt-edged security.

Hilary, immersed already in one of her long ironic conversations with herself about Boston, stopped in full flight, to ask herself, but *why* the irony? What had been wrong? Why when they were so impeccable, were they also just faintly ridiculous? Why when so noble, was some elusive value just lacking . . . , this was the mystery. Was it that they lacked the aristocratic virtue of treating serious things lightly and light things seriously? Despite the elaborate family jokes and rites, the general atmosphere *was* frightfully earnest, and in a strange way, devitalized. There were times when she felt she loomed over her parents like some larger fiercer kind of animal, and where had she come from then, a sport from some ancestor, some wild Welshman from the eighteenth century?

"I am nobody's child," she had shouted at her mother once in a fury. "I'm nothing like you or Pa and being like you would kill me!"

"Well, you're not Pallas Athene, that's sure," her mother

had said with a touch of acerbity. "I labored twenty-four hours to bring you into the world, my girl."

"And after all that you wanted a boy!"

"I never said so."

"You must have—anybody would." Hilary was relentless.

"*I* wanted a girl," her father said in his slightly teasing gentle voice, "so you really cannot pretend whatever you are trying to pretend this time."

"I wanted to *be* a boy, I guess," Hilary had granted, standing at the window in the Beacon Street upstairs library and looking out on four or five boys of about her own age having a fierce snowball fight in the street. Her father could tame her when no one else could, tame her by his gentleness, by that quizzical look round his eyes when he looked at her; although he was so shy, she felt his love as an absolute certainty.

With her mother it was so much more complicated . . . self-aware, terrified perhaps of spoiling an only child, punishing them both by refusing to give in to what she would have called mawkishness. Tenderness was only safe if given or received by the sick in bed and no wonder Hilary spent such large numbers of weeks as a child being ill! No wonder she had reacted so violently all her life to the fear of feeling, and to the fury who attended it, the sense of guilt. The wonderful thing about the English society into which Hilary had moved when she married Adrian was the total absence of this cramped and cramping sense of duty. It was a larger air; things could be taken for granted; money, power, could be taken for granted. The relief it had been!

But when Hilary thought of her mother, the image was always of her sitting at the small desk in her bedroom, overwhelmed by what she had failed to accomplish, paying for every moment of pleasure with hours of self-castigating good works, driven to visit hospitals, driven to do far more than she needed to about opening and closing summer houses and camps, so she radiated anxiety and tension. Yet this image must be crossed with another, equally valid, of her mother coming down the staircase on her way out to dinner, looking brilliant, a little flushed, a plain woman who could suddenly become a beauty, who, unlike her daughter, flourished in social situations, loved good conversation with a passion, enjoyed pitting her mind and her personality against those of her peers—a woman whom men admired and (Hilary suspected) whom more than one had been more than a little in love with, a woman who could flirt with the man on her left and then with the man on her right, but who would have been horrified to be taken seriously by either of them.

Hilary, leaning over the banisters, was melted by the apparition, the exquisite pale pink Worth dress, the subdued excitement in her mother's voice, as she asked her husband,

"Do I look all right, dear?"

"Smashing!"

"I am not quite sure about the pink. . . . It doesn't look too young?"

Hilary had run down the stairs and thrown her arms around her mother. "Oh you smell delicious!"

"Careful, Hilary, don't crumple me." But was it, old Hilary wondered, as the scene came into focus with the felt pang intact, that Ma was afraid of being crumpled, or afraid of the intensity with which she felt herself being hugged? She drove me into the arms of governesses, teachers, strangers . . . anyone who provided escape from the tightly controlled shining surface, the prison anyone who could let in a little air.

"What is wrong with our parents?" Hilary remembered asking Nancy one day.

"We never get enough to eat!" The answer was so immediate and so true, that they fell into a fit of hysterical giggles. Frugality was one of the esteemed values in this particular Boston. (Later Hilary was amazed to discover that there were Cabots and Hallowells who ate exceedingly well and seemed to feel no guilt about enjoying food.) As it was, Hilary and Nancy spent a good part of their allowances, twenty-five cents a week, eating banana splits in a drugstore.

"Also they go away too much. . . . They're always going away and leaving us with Hellish governesses. You must admit, Hilary, it's *inhuman!*" They were at the age, about thirteen, when every other word was spoken with emphasis and when they wrote letters, one underlining was seldom sufficient.

"Inhuman," Hilary murmured as she lay on her side, thinking the word over. Her parents would surely have

[65

been amazed that such a word could be seriously used. But had they had even an inkling of what the constant displacement, the endless trips to Europe did to a child? What being out of school for a year did to one at fourteen, for instance? And coming back to find oneself almost a total stranger to girls who had had a whole life without you, in that year away? But of course what they valued above all was "culture." (How Hilary had hated the word!) It seemed far more important than physical or psychic comfort ever could. Frugality, industry, kindness, and never losing your temper, those were the values—those, and "culture," a real and discriminating love of the arts. Yes, she had to admit that it was discriminating, and more, even passionate. Life at one remove could be allowed to be passionate. And Hilary smiled, wondering whether the massed gray heads and little furs at the Friday afternoon symphony had not perhaps concealed frustrated emotional drunkards who drank music as if it were liquor. Well, no doubt it all had a keen edge. Her mother, of course, had a very keen edge indeed, but she was not comfortable. One did not hug her. "Inhuman" then because it was the physical world which was continuously denied, which was somehow disgusting, giving in to it in any way being a sign of weakness. The one exception was the summer, Sorrento, when a certain amount of physical hardship no doubt justified the delight in picnics, swimming in the freezing water, tennis, and reading aloud. If there had been a root at all, it was Sorrento, the sea. There, Hilary considered, they had lived as total human beings, not split up into guilt, culture, and self-denial.

But what had they been to each other? she wondered for the millionth time about her parents. Had they been a real comfort to each other, or had her mother taken her distaste for physical things to bed? "It is that!" Hilary sat up in bed and ate the rest of her sandwich in a famished kind of way. She saw for the first time really what the flaw had been, what the missing value was in the etherial world where she had grown up. It was the fact that all bodily functions were regarded as slightly indelicate, the body it-self a donkey one carried about and treated with disdain. It was greedy to enjoy food; it was soft to enjoy a comfor-table bed, and ordinary physical needs such as evacuating induced real shame. . . , so under all the splendid riches there was a fundamental poverty, a distortion, which could have made me a cripple, Hilary thought. She sup-posed that what had saved her was the summers at Sor-rento . . . but, what did she still have to track down, lost somewhere at the bottom of all her musing like a shining pebble of truth? The lilacs! Now the vision rose up of her mother in the garden, her hands and face scratched and dirty for she had been pruning roses, with a look of extreme sensuous delight as she lifted one dark red rose and buried her nose in it. So, no doubt, she had done with the lilacs, bending them down as if to eat their sweetness. Her mother had touched each single flower with a kind of tenderness she gave to nothing else, and during one summer of extended drought, she had herself seemed to wither, had lain in the dark, Hilary remembered complaining of migraine, because she could not bear to watch her garden dying of thirst. The vision stayed there, suspended like some angel over her head. So her mother had after all known what the senses can give, delight so sharp that it is poignant. Am I the child of passionate love? Hilary asked herself, hoping wildly that it might be so. But she would never know. All personal letters were solemnly burnt by her mother in an incinerator at the point, some years before her death. By then Hilary was an established novelist and poet. Was this act of her mother's a final act of rejection? A defence? What was she protecting? Natural reticence before the formidable public life of an only daughter? . . . I did all the wrong things, Hilary thought, despair rising in her throat. "You are not like us," her mother had said with a queer little gesture half tender, half dismayed, when Hilary's first novel came out. "I feel I do not know you any more."

Hilary suppressed the answer: you never have. You have been so busy trying to mould me to some image you have in your head, that you never considered who or what I might be in myself.

Yet when her mother received compliments from members of the Nucleus Club, she could not help showing that she was pleased and proud. "Our duckling has turned into a swan," she would say, and laugh in a self-deprecating way. "It is so very odd. . . . Hilary has become a prima donna, that funny little awkward girl covered with mosquito bites." The accolade could never be given simply and outright to any one of one's family; that would have seemed arrogant.

Once her father had almost come to the point of speaking. They were riding together, an early morning ride, taken in the hope of seeing two horned owls who were nesting at the end of the point. Delicious early morning chill and the smell of pine and wild roses and salt!

Hilary heard his dry nervous cough, always the announcement that he had come to the point of uttering. They were walking the horses side by side.

"I wonder . . . ," he said, and Hilary held her breath. "I do wonder how you have come to know all that you seem to know—about life. It makes me feel. . . ." But at this point he was overcome by shyness and roused his mount to a trot, so easy he was, at home in the saddle, so baffled by the human situation.

Hilary that time made an attempt to answer the unasked question.

"I knew enough when I was fifteen to write that book."

Her father chuckled. "Boarding schools must be rather more illuminating places than we had imagined."

"Anyone who is going to be a writer knows enough at fifteen to write several novels," Hilary said crossly. "It's too bad I'm a writer. I should have been a painter. Painters get away with murder, and nobody minds."

"Well!" Her father drew up old Baldy to a halt and gave her a smile of great relief. He had discovered a way to fit her in, after all. "I suppose you must have inherited all this from your Great Aunt Ida."

"She who ended her days at McLean?" Hilary laughed.

[69

"Honestly, do I have to fit into the family tree like a bird into some pre-planned nest? Why can't I be myself? Why do I have to be *like* that insane old woman, who was a bad painter—we might as well face it!"

"Your Aunt Ida had considerable talent, Hilary. You forget that she is hung in the Boston Museum of Fine Arts."

"In the cellar, by now."

"You are being rude."

Hilary flushed and galloped off. Better to get right away fast, than to utter the accumulated bitterness of all the years. When she had calmed down, Hilary felt shame; she had spoken cynically and without compassion of an old woman whom she loved. Aunt Ida had given her her first pair of opera glasses; she had talked to her as if she were a human being, not a child; and when she had been locked up ("Aunt Ida is very ill," she was told, "and in a hospital"), Hilary at twelve had felt real grief. The old woman had tried to commit suicide—this fact oozed out somehow from under the pretenses. Then she was buried alive, and one more item was added to Alice Frothingham's lists of "things to do," the weekly visit to McLean with books and flowers, with paints and canvases, for there had been times when Aunt Ida moved from depression to elation and could for brief periods paint again. Hilary had not been allowed to see her. Perhaps they imagined that insanity was contagious.

Oh, the awful tears had begun to flow out of her eyes, just as they had that day years ago when she had turned her horse back and managed to say, "I loved Aunt Ida, and I'm glad if I can be like her. . . . She was *human.*"

"Well," and her father coughed, "no need to be upset, Hilary. I was only saying that there does seem to be a streak of talent in the family." And that was that.

That was that then, but now after her troubled night, and in her state of suspense and tension before the interview, it seemed as if all Hilary's feeling about her parents was dangerously close to the surface again. If only once they could have been proud, really and wholeheartedly proud, she thought. What I wanted and never got from them was *recognition.* But even fame seemed to them suspect; like the rich who spent money, it was too obvious to be quite appropriate to their way of life.

You can't break the mould and also be consoled for breaking it, old fool! Be realistic—every book you published must have caused them embarassment and dismay. Yet the cry that escaped her lips, as she searched for the handkerchief in her pocket was, "Mother! Father!" Does the mourning for parents ever end? she asked herself, blowing her nose, and resting her eyes on the quiet green light in the room. Searingly, excruciatingly private, this pain, yet she suspected that it might be the universal condition. Children have to hurt their parents or die, have to break themselves off, whatever the cost, even though the wound never heals.

Nevertheless, young Hilary reminded old Hilary, you have not after all done too badly, old thing. You did not break down like Aunt Ida; you kept going; you have

[71

worked hard, and you have made a garden, which would have pleased your mother; and once in a while you have even been able to be of some use to another human being— Mar for instance. Now pull yourself together! Make like a genius (young Hilary enjoyed using slang) and get some armor on.

The armor she decided on, after some fidgeting about in the closet, was a violet suede jacket, a gray tweed skirt, and a pale pink silk blouse with an open collar, to which she pinned a diamond fox with a ruby eye which Aunt Ida had left her in her will. There remained only to slip on some rather elegant slippers. She did rather admire her small feet, even if from there on up there was disintegration.

It was three o'clock, and she must dig out that list of things not to forget on the tea tray. Also remember to light the fire in the big room. The spring inside her which had gone slack in the middle of the afternoon—even on ordinary days it was apt to—began to coil itself up and tighten.

"It's going to be fun, old thing!"

Interlude: the interviewers

Peter Selversen and Jenny
Hare were rushing toward Hil-
ary in a rented Volkswagen as Route 128 unwound itself, a
long wide ribbon up and down hills. Nerved up, as the
journey from New York neared its end, they were acutely
aware of what they saw around them.

The May day had kept its freshness, and at three o'clock
still retained the quality of stained glass; they moved
through a huge iridescent bubble of fresh greens and reds
against a transparent blue sky without a cloud. Every-
where the lilac had burst into clusters of pale green
pointed leaves; the small estuaries and tidal rivers floated
the sky. For the moment they were talked out, full of what
they were seeing and of the quarry before them, expectancy layered over conjecture, and the magic of the day it-

self layered over that; what would there have been to say? Besides they were still in the stage of "making conversation"; they had met only the week before, in order to prepare the interview.

The editors of *The Review* felt that it might be a good idea to have a woman along, and picked Jenny because she was George's girl friend (he was associate editor); she was not a poet, but she had won an O. Henry Award for a short story. She was sufficiently professional but had no axe to grind, and she was young. They hoped that the old writer would open up to a young woman, that Jenny might be able to pose certain questions more gracefully than Peter could.

He, of course, was the star performer in the act; this particular kind of interview, related entirely to the work itself, serious and probing, had become his stock in trade. Many people subscribed to the magazine only for the sake of these exemplary exercises in tact and persuasion; indeed it was fascinating to watch "great writers" unbutton about their art, speak with frankness about their problems as *writers.* And Peter had realized from the beginning that even the very famous are surprised and delighted when it becomes clear that they have been read with the greatest sensitivity and attention, and that when they speak they are (for a change) being listened to. But he had rarely approached such an occasion knowing so little of a personal nature. No recent photograph of F. Hilary Stevens had been available; and almost no biographical material; the barest facts in *Who's Who* (though she was not one of those who conceal their age); and, of course, the books themselves . . . two novels, and nine volumes of poems, mostly out of print, except for the last, this late success, the reason for the interview. He had been surprised himself to discover what a good poet she was, surprised and a little ashamed. And it was of this he was thinking, as he swerved in and out around lumbering trucks . . . of the ironies and the cruelties of what people called "the writing game," the Olympic game of the spirit where so often the best do not win, at least in their lifetime. What gusto and conviction F. Hilary Stevens must have to break out of the tomb at seventy and thumb her nose at the critics and anthologists who had buried her alive! Very possibly he and Jenny would now meet the pent-up aggressions and bitterness. Certainly the poems did not suggest a mild old party! Well, it would be interesting. . . .

It was Peter's genius that he was always and omnivorously "interested." Now he was interested not only in the quarry coming into view in an hour but also in the young woman at his side, hands clasped tightly on her knees, almost too conscious of her responsibilities.

"O.K., Jenny?"

"O.K.," she answered without taking her eyes from the road. "I'm looking. It all feels so safe and pretty, but I suppose every one of those little factories is busily making some sort of infernal machine, right beside an old house where Hawthorne might have lived. New England is *so* peculiar. . . ." He was aware that this was Jenny's first foray North of Boston. Like many New Yorkers, she came from the Middle West, Indianapolis, if he remembered, and Peter had a gift for remembering.

"When I was at Harvard, this was still open country—ten years ago—cows lying around. It's become a vast suburb. I hardly recognize anything. Just over there, for instance, used to be a turkey farm!" It was now a colony of cheap pink-and-white frame houses, adjacent to a factory. "Peculiar?"

"Well, compared to the countryside I know best around Indianapolis it *is* higgledy-piggledy, cultivated, inhabited, layer over layer of different kinds of life. There's no stretch where you see the same thing for more than a minute, it seems to me. That's what's peculiar."

"Yankee ingenuity at work! Those people built the clipper ships, and now they are busily building computers, or what have you!"

"Those people, you say—as if they were a race apart!"

"Yet they are actually mostly Italians, Greeks, Irish, I expect."

"Not in that house!" They flashed past a yellow clapboard house with a large barn attached to it, and a lovely oval fanlight over the door. "There's the stamp of elegance; you can't escape it. Even the old dories lying upside down over there in the mud have an air about them. One *recognizes* it, Peter . . . ," and then she asked, "What will F. Hilary Stevens be like, do you suppose?"

"Not to be pinned down to this landscape is my guess. She's been a wanderer, an oddity. She married an Englishman, lived abroad most of her life, came back here in her late fifties. . . . It's complex."

"I'm scared," Jenny said and, having admitted it, at last unclasped her hands.

"There has to be an edge or nothing happens. I suppose these interviews are a kind of collision."

"Head-on?" And Jenny laughed on the wave of excitement, and also on the wave of her pleasure in him. She had got fond of him, she suddenly discovered, fond of his pockmarked face, his deep-set dark eyes, his way of speaking in rushes as if a certain amount of contained pressure had to be released. She sensed that he had the detachment and kindness of the person who is by nature an observer rather than an actor. He would never be conflicted, rent in two as she was most of the time. He could afford to be genial in a way that she could not. He was, indeed, an endearing companion.

"Yes, in a way, head-on. We are rolling toward her at sixty, and no doubt she is, inside herself, approaching us at the same speed."

Was he deliberately building up the tension in himself, Jenny wondered? She found the image of F. Hilary Stevens hurtling toward them like some jinni out of a bottle, terrifying.

"Light me a cigarette, will you?" As he turned to take it, he noticed the thin line of sweat on Jenny's upper lip, and it touched him. He had been rather put off at first by her moonlike face, gray eyes magnified behind glasses, had pigeonholed her as one of those ambitious women who live from the neck up. But here was total response. The poor kid was scared.

"I find it comforting that she is old," he said.

"Why?"

"I suppose I have a thing about old women. Their characters may be rather stylized, but once you get past mannerism, they are, well? how to put it? Transparent. It isn't worth it any longer to wear a mask."

"I suppose young people do; I suppose you are right," Jenny resisted the temptation to argue this. "Children and old people. They are either emerging or have emerged. They are not in the middle battling it out." She lit a cigarette for herself and took a puff, thinking this over. "I suppose you and I do wear masks." She gave him a mischievous, sidelong glance.

"Only compare for a second what you really feel like and what you show to the world! Sheer self-protection, Jenny. Sometimes I think one has a different mask or shield, or whatever it is, for every relationship. I fear I do."

"And you think F. Hilary Stevens doesn't? Don't forget that the people she could feel at ease with must be dying out, the real people."

"Real people?"

"Her contemporaries, friends—also those she admired, longed to be like, her own masters."

"Her masters were dead when she began. She goes right back to Wyatt, Skelton—and in certain odd moments to Traherne."

"Anyway I don't suppose a poet *can* wear a mask. How I

envy her being a poet!"

"You think it's easier?"

"Don't pounce! You scare me."

"I'm interested, Jenny," he pleaded. Talk to a writer about writing and invisible hackles begin to rise. God knows, he had observed it often enough: *noli me tangere.*

"I'm sorry." The fact was that she was nervy enough any way and the imminent ordeal made her more so. "Perhaps it is that poets are accepted as slightly mad to begin with. But I am so tired of being treated like a threat, some sort of Medusa image. *You* know, Peter! I am not making this up, am I?"

"Making what up?"

"I have seen people freeze when they hear I am a writer —that, or they pour out their life story and tell you it is a gift and you can use it for your next novel! Or—even worse—they imagine you are so eager for experience that they can make a pass and get away with it. . . . You are never, never treated just as a woman. . . ."

"Isn't the thing maybe that you are *not* just a woman?" Peter asked gently. "And my guess is that you don't want to be."

"It's so lonely, Peter, if you only knew!" She wondered with excruciating anxiety now whether he and George had talked about her. She had no idea what these two would be like together alone, in their world, the impenetrable masculine world. "Say something!"

"I'm thinking." He sensed the spiral of intensity, which so often in women coiled itself up, only to loose itself finally in tears, beginning its nerve-wracking ascension, and he was afraid. It would never do for her to arrive at their destination in a state of inner dishevelment. He was nervous of the furies who seemed at the moment to be swooping down over their heads. "I guess women pay a pretty high price for whatever talents they have. I guess it's harder for them than it is for a man, always."

"But you haven't answered! You don't want to!"

He gave her his serious smile, "You've got me in a corner. What makes you think I know?"

"I think maybe you like women," she said. It was her opinion that Geroge really did not like them. He was trying to fall in love, to catch it from her, but the Hell was that she knew and he knew that so far the operation had not been successful.

"Yes," Peter said. "I do. I should have thought that a rather common masculine characteristic, like having to shave." He chuckled.

"I think, for a lot of men, women *loom,*" she said sadly.

"Gods who have to be propitiated with human sacrifice?" He waited for her laugh and then saw that she was not laughing.

"I meant that as a joke, Jenny, let's not be so serious," he squeezed her hand fraternally.

"I have to be serious about this. I can't help it. It's my life after all." She pulled her hand away. "I want to marry, Peter, and have children, and a house, and a dog, and several cats. I want to be treated like a human being and to *be* a human being, don't you see?"

Peter accelerated and passed two huge trucks. The spurt of speed suggested impatience, and Jenny watched him out of the corner of her eye, in a sort of desperation.

"It's all right for a man to have work and to be married, but when a woman does, it's a threat."

"Maybe a man wants a woman to be his woman, and not some art's woman . . . maybe it makes him feel insecure," he hazarded.

"What about F. Hilary Stevens then?" she asked aggressively. "She got married."

"Her husband died young—we can't know."

"Colette had three husbands!"

"Exactly!" For the first time Peter felt needled and cross. "It wasn't the sort of life you have just described so nostalgically, was it? A writer's life is obsessed, driven, in the hands of powers he can hardly control himself. Writing must seem often the only reality. I just don't believe you can do it with your right hand while your left hand rocks a cradle, Jenny!"

"But how can you be a good writer and not live? How do you ever know?"

"How did we ever get into this?" he asked the air, for Jenny's head was turned toward the woods. "I have an idea your questions had better wait for the horse's mouth. We should be there soon."

"How soon?"

"Don't panic. Just ferret about in my briefcase and find that yellow sheet with all the directions and tell me what it says. We must be close to Gloucester now."

Jenny found the crumpled piece of paper, was amused to discover that F. Hilary Stevens' typing was as erratic as her own. "It says, keep going past Gloucester and Rockport around Cape Ann, until you come to Folly Cove. At Folly Cove turn left on a rough unpaved road and keep going past two abandoned quarries to the end! . . . . Folly Cove? Abandoned quarries? How symbolic can you get? She's fooling." Jenny felt laughter rising in her, instead of the tears she had so feared would overcome her. And this bubble of laughter grew and grew and became irresistible. Peter chortled beside her, occasionally gasping "Folly Cove" and "quarries," as relieved as Jenny was to be out of the dangerous passage. The furies had gone away.

Now they drove through delicious waves of salt air; it came and went, tantalizing, and after they had turned away from the classic prettiness of Rockport, there were occasional glimpses of the ocean, around a bend, or back of a house. It lay there, stretched silk on this windless day, perfectly serene, silencing the city-bred, opulent background to the tight white houses.

"Oh Peter, do stop! I want to look. . . ."

He turned off the road by an old stone pier, beside a lobster joint still boarded up for the winter. They got out and walked down to the end of the pier, taking deep breaths of the air, relieved to break for the moment the inexorable momentum of the drive.

"Imagine *living* here!" Jenny said lifting her face to the air as if to drink it.

"Rock, kelp, waves, light. . . ."

"Too much light. Too open. I could never utter a word! What could one say in front of this?" But Peter had bent his head and was not really listening. He walked off by himself then, and when he came back, said, concluding a train of thought, "Listen, Jenny, let's be clear about one thing. I want you to keep in mind that as I see it, the crux of this interview has to do with the whole creative thing for a woman poet."

"Why not just a *poet?* Why haul in the woman part?"

"Listen, porcupine, keep those quills down for a second, will you? You said a while ago that it was harder to be a woman writer."

"*You* said it!"

"O.K., I said it. That's not what I'm talking about anyway. What seems to me valid and interesting is the question posited at such huge length by Robert Graves in *The White Goddess*—who and what is the Muse? Here we have a poet who has gone on writing poems long after the Muse, at least in a personal incarnation, has become irrelevant. What sustains the intensity? Is there a White God?" he asked and immediately felt how funny it sounded. They both laughed.

"Of course not!"

"Well then. . . ."

Jenny looked out to sea. "Maybe Aphrodite rises from the waves now and then. . . ."

Peter looked at his watch. "Come on!" he called back, running to the car. "We'll be late."

They were, actually, close to the cove, though they

[83

could not see it, around the next point. It lay there, bounded on both sides by monumental rocks, shining and still. But in hot pursuit of the gods, they hardly looked. Besides, it was necessary almost at once to turn up the "rough" road on the left. Rough it was; it looked as if it had been created by a giant throwing rocks down a dry brook-bed, and Peter and Jenny were fiercely jolted. On the left they recognized one of the quarries, now a dark green pool at the foot of a steep cliff; clumps of iris around the lower edge gave it the look of a Japanese garden. They passed a shuttered clapboard house, still sealed up for winter. A bone-shaking crack brought "Damn!" to Peter's lips.

"What was that?"

"A rock. I just hope it didn't crack the axle."

The car shuddered, but managed to grip the uneven surface again, and plunged upwards past some unattractive scrub, black birch, and locusts, past an overgrown apple orchard, and finally past a much larger quarry on the right, it too filled with water.

The quarries gave a classic air to the otherwise untamed landscape; the combination, it occurred to Jenny, did seem to have some relation to the poems. But it was impossible to speak at the moment because of the jolts.

"Look, there it is!" and Peter swung in through a narrow drive between two giant clumps of lilac and out into a circle in front of the house. Groups of daffodil and narcissus were in flower below a broken down stone wall. The house itself, not clapboard as they had somehow expected, but gray fieldstone, with white trim at the windows and a bright blue door, was more of an "estate" than Jenny at least had imagined it would be. She felt extremely nervous, as Peter stopped the car. In silence they gathered up notebooks and handbags, gently closed the car doors, performing these actions as if on tiptoe, very much aware of the possibility that they were being observed. They walked up to the blue door and Peter pulled the old-fashioned door bell. Inside they could hear a faint tinkle, so faint, and without reverberation, that it seemed as if the house might be empty.

"What if . . . ," Jenny whispered.

Part II: the interview

Before Jenny could finish her sentence, the door opened in their faces. They towered there like awkward giants looking down at the small stooped personage looking up at them, head a little on one side, who said in a surprisingly resonant voice to come from so frail a vessel.

"So it's you! Do come in. You must be tired after your long journey. Planes are exhausting, I always feel; one can't settle in somehow."

F. Hilary Stevens did not look as Jenny expected her to look and was far less formidable than she had imagined. The fine childlike hair, cut short to cover the head as closely as a bird's feathers, was disarming; disarming, too, one lock allowed to fall over the narrow forehead at a slightly rakish angle. Below this cap, the eyebrows, pale and tufted, the sharply boned nose, the penetrating light-gray eyes, half-hooded under sensitized drooping lids, gave her an owlish look. But no one could have called this extraordinary face a mask, even an owl-mask, it was far too mobile.

"You are Miss Hare, I presume? And this is Mr. Silverstone."

"Selversen."

They shook hands. It was apparent that whatever went on inside F. Hilary Stevens she would have to be called a lady.

"Selversen, is it? Swedish or Danish. I sometimes think that people should always be named for animals. Then one might remember—Hare, for instance, is not forgettable. Perfect name for a writer, I should imagine, those wild eyes, and not to be tamed. Still, you look quite calm, Miss Hare. Would you like to wash?"

"Yes, thank you."

"Up one flight, and to your left. You may use the downstairs facilities, if you will," and she waved Peter toward a door under the stairs. "You will find me in the big room," she called to the disappearing two.

Each was glad of the moment in which to register the complete sensation, the first—always so significant—impact, and to do it alone. Peter had caught at once an impression of a person advancing and retreating at the same instant, both transparent and secret, like her face, a person in continuous dialogue with herself. In the bathroom he hummed with excitement.

[87

Jenny had no time to define what she had seen, for when she opened her bathroom door she was faced by a wall of photographs and pencil sketches, and scanned them rapidly, thinking, I must manage to come back here again before we leave. There was a faded brown photograph of a British officer, a riding crop in one hand. Captain Stevens, no doubt. There was an old man in a beret with a thick moustache like Joffre's, in workmen's corduroys, standing against an old stone wall. Beside him, in an oval gold frame, a pastel sketch of a woman in a huge Edwardian plumed hat, leaning on a closed parasol, her face bent toward a rose bush, so one caught only a tantalizing glimpse. There was a charming photograph of Elinor Wylie standing in a doorway, smiling; one of Mary Garden lying on a chaise longue, and beside it several other actresses or singers whom Jenny failed to recognize. No one on that wall can be under eighty now, and most of them must be dead, she thought. And it gave her a queer sensation; the woman waiting downstairs was so alive, so much in command, yet what a complex past a human being drags behind him by the time he is in his seventies . . . all those faces, all those lives, all one's life, so much of it still undigested, so many doors closed on things one might rather not look back on, so much still troubling (but I am reading myself into this, and none of it may be true). Did F. Hilary Stevens suffer guilt? Did she weep in the night? Or did her generation itself provide her with a kind of immunity, moulded as she had been before World War I, and before Freud? But, after all, photographs freeze the current of life. It was there waiting downstairs, the electric current.

When Jenny walked into the big room, Peter was standing with his back to the open fire, looking very much at home.

"I couldn't tear myself away from all those people," she said.

"What a crew! Antediluvian!" Hilary Stevens gave a light apologetic laugh. "Never look at 'em, don't you know?" Then, as if to herself, "Know them by heart. It's a mistake to put up photographs. They go dead on you."

"What have I missed?" Peter asked.

"Oh, people . . . photographs . . . all the people!" F. Hilary Stevens waved them away like so many ghosts whose presence she took for granted, who, perhaps, did not interest her. "I put them up when I first moved in, ten years ago, staking my claim, as it were, but since that day I've hardly looked at them." Mrs. Stevens was sitting in the wing chair by the fireplace. The strong afternoon light sharpened the planes of her face; she looked her age. "How do you take your tea, Miss Hare?"

"Strong, with sugar and milk, please."

"Americans like lemon. I have a lemon, just in case, but of course good English tea requires milk. Miss Hare is a sensible person," she announced to Peter, with evident satisfaction.

"Very sensible," said Peter, giving Jenny an amused look, "very sensible indeed."

F. Hilary Stevens caught the glance, and pounced, "No

irony, please. There is nothing so irritating—so fashion-
able too. I am so tired of irony." She deftly poured the tea
as she spoke, giving Peter a mischievous smile as she
handed him the cup to pass to Jenny, "Or is it that I am
afraid of it?" she asked the air, resuming the dialogue with
herself. "It kills poetry perhaps."

"Perhaps . . . ," Peter ventured as a question.

"You're not sure?" She laughed again. "Neither am I!
The minute one utters a certainty, the opposite comes to
mind." The withdrawal was complete. She was not to be
drawn so soon. "And your tea, Mr. . . . Selversen?"

"Milk, please. Who would dare say lemon?"

"Why not? You're not sensible, are you? Men don't have
to be."

"Do women?" Jenny asked.

"Of course, naturally. Women have to deal with the
things men in their wildness and genius have invented.
It's clear as daylight." The eyes hooded themselves while
F. Hilary Stevens poured her own cup, by now strong, and
added a lashing of milk. "Pass the sandwiches, if you
would be so good," she said to Peter, and to Jenny, or to
herself, murmured, "Anchovy. I spent hours slicing
through thick slices of bread to achieve a reasonable fac-
simile of a sandwich. You can have no idea," she turned to
Peter with her most charming smile, "how sensible women
have to learn to be."

"And if they are wild and genius-y, what then?" Peter
asked as he offered the plate—gold-edged, wreathed in
roses, and piled high with elegant little sandwiches—to

Jenny.

"Then. . . ." The pause was held as by a rather fine actress. But in mid-air, she changed her mind. "I don't know. I really don't know." She stuffed half a sandwich in her mouth. When she had swallowed it, she asked, "Will you tell me when the interview begins? I feel rather nervous. I was not able to work very well this morning, so many questions, probable or improbable, hovered in the air. I am not good at answering other people's questions," she dared them. "So often they seem irrelevant."

"Yes, I know." Peter sat down and crossed his legs, deliberately unhurried. "We'll try to be relevant, as relevant as we can. But if you like, you could both ask the questions and give the answers; we have no rules. In fact, what a good idea! That would relieve us of all responsibility!"

"Oh, I am not responsible—God forbid!" Then she added, obviously enjoying herself, "It was just contemplating your responsibility that made me nervous this morning."

"We were dreadfully nervous," Jenny said.

"Really?" The gray eyes narrowed. "But it's your job, after all; you are used to it, aren't you?"

"You don't get 'used to' genius," Peter said gently. "No interview in my experience has been in any way like any other."

"Mmmm," Mrs. Stevens tasted this remark with evident pleasure and then set the pleasure aside with a shake of her head, "Let me say at once that I have no illusions about my 'genius.' " She gazed out at the sea and half closed her eyes. "A small, accurate talent, exploited to the limit, let us be quite clear about *that!*" Then she added, perhaps unaware that she had spoken aloud, "Damn it!" Opened her eyes wide, and turned back to the tray before her. "Have some more tea. When does the interview begin?"

"Whenever you choose, looking back, to have had it begin," Peter said, passing his cup.

"I am to be my own censor?"

"Would you dislike that?"

"Poetry writing, I sometimes think, is nothing but self-censorship. I spend my life disciplining the impulse, when the impulse is there. But I sometimes wonder whether if I had quelled the censor, I might not have done better. Women are afraid of their daemon, want to control it, make it sensible like themselves." She turned to Jenny who was grateful to be included. She had felt as if she were watching a fast ping-pong game and, as a player, was hardly in the league. "Do you agree, Miss Hare?"

"Oh yes! I suppose I'm a fool to think it should get easier as one gets older."

"Nothing gets easier as one gets older. Everything is harder, even buttoning one's slipper!" Jenny instinctively looked down to note the elegant slippers, bronze, with one button. And Miss Stevens followed her eyes. "It's the stooping," she explained. "The trouble is that one becomes a kind of donkey." And she laughed. "Yet . . . ," the dialogue set itself up again, "I suppose the donkey teaches one a few things, to handle oneself with less waste of energy, for instance. There is less energy to waste, don't you know? Writing poems is always easy and always very hard at the same time—at any age."

"In what way easy, Mrs. Stevens?" Peter placed his cup and saucer down with a click on the tray. The click did something to the atmosphere—he had meant it to.

"The interview begins here," said F. Hilary Stevens, settling back into her chair, and almost entirely closing her eyes. "Easy . . . hard . . . ," she murmured. "Easy because one can't do it at all unless one is propelled. Set in motion, as it were. Until there is momentum. Elusive," she opened her eyes and smiled. "I have sometimes raced the motor for hours and found I was standing still. Something went agley. The darn thing didn't start."

"You weren't in gear," Peter suggested.

"Precisely. How does one get in gear? What does it?"

"Possibly that is the question we had most in mind to ask," Peter exchanged a glance with Jenny, a glance of delight and of triumph, then added soberly. "But just because it is *the* question, I suggest we leave it for a moment and come back to it through the logical sequence of your work." He took out a pad and laid it on his knee. F. Hilary Stevens watched him with a slightly mocking, slightly nervous look which he caught as he lifted his head. "Is that agreeable to you, Mrs. Stevens?"

"I am delivered up, lock, stock, and barrel."

"May we go back a bit before returning to the poems? At twenty-three you made a tremendous hit with a first novel, not inappropriately called *The Bull's Eye*. Yet, despite your success, you broke the mould, and shortly afterwards published poems and only poems for many years. Would you like to talk about this?"

F. Hilary Stevens sat back in her chair, sitting up very straight. The tension was visible. "It's harder than you might think to talk about it. Give me a minute." Again she looked out beyond them to the sea. "It was, I must confess, a painful experience. I got in beyond my depth. Oh, I had written honestly enough, but the last thing I had wanted or imagined was a *succès de scandale*. It was a shock." She turned to Jenny with a rather shy smile, as if asking for the first time for help.

"It's such a spontaneous book," Jenny plunged in, encouraged by the unspoken plea. "So fresh—it made me think of a brilliant water color. But I suppose people were shocked because you talked about things like women falling in love with each other, took this for granted, set it in its place; and the love affair with the young man is awfully good."

"You are kind. . . ." But Mrs. Stevens' attention was clearly absorbed elsewhere. "I know," she said, "I've got it! *Rosenkavalier!*" She looked from one to the other of them, and drew a blank. "The ambiguity, don't you see? That's what made it sell! I didn't know quite what I was doing myself. Oh, if I could have written that book twenty five years later, then it might have been something!" The tone changed; she leaned her chin on one hand and went into the familiar dialogue with herself. "Yet one writes to find out. I suppose I dislike the book because it seems to me now superficial, not worthy of its subject. I never looked

Medusa in the face."

"You forget that you had a style!" Peter said.

"Oh well, these self-intoxicated explosions may have some significance—," she brushed Peter's praise aside. But perhaps it had been relieving. For the first time since their arrival, she seemed perfectly natural, as she said, "I mean to be honest with you. That is why you have come, to help me to be honest, is it not?"

"I hardly think we imagined ourselves in that role," Peter said gravely, but there was a twinkle in his eye.

"I should never have let you come if I had not imagined that a benefit would ensue. It is possible," Mrs. Stevens said, "that I feel so strongly about that book because I have been trying to elude it all these years. You could never guess what it really sprang from, nor shall I tell you." She swallowed a secret smile. "That is irrelevant."

"I wonder . . . ," Peter leaned forward, but she had already escaped him, and was standing at the French windows at the other end of the room, hands in the pockets of her purple jacket, looking out.

Peter made some quick notes on his pad, and Jenny looked around the big formal room, taking it in for the first time, since she had until now been wholly concentrated on the presence of F. Hilary Stevens herself. She noted pale gray walls, a big old-fashioned sofa covered in a chintzy faded rose pattern, the eighteenth century mantelpiece which bore several amusing bibelots, a lustre jug, a Burmese duck covered in gold leaf, a Chelsea shepherdess with a lamb; over the mantle her eyes came to rest on a pencil sketch by Sargent of a person whom Jenny at first took to be a young man in a velvet jacket with a Byronic, open white collar, and then suddenly recognized as Mrs. Stevens herself. She rose to decipher the date, 1920, contemporaneous then with the success of the novel. Sargent had caught well the gleam of mischief, of self-mockery, which had remained characteristic of his subject. It was clear that she had always been a charmer, and knew it.

The other paintings in the room enhanced the atmosphere of light, order, and peace: two French impressionists, one of an apple orchard in flower, and the other of women transplanting lettuce in a vegetable garden dappled with light and shadow. There was a pot of blue hyacinths on the long refectory table, and a few daffodils had been arranged to charming effect in a Venetian glass under a Venetian mirror. Clearly this was not a room where anyone did any writing. A little cool, it might have felt, but for the glow of the wood fire, and the tea tray abandoned there like a still life among them. Yet, despite the coolness and order, the room communicated a sense of life with a keen edge. The house was full of presences; she who lived here alone was surrounded by angels or ghosts, perhaps by both. Yes, it had an atmosphere like its creator, Jenny decided, of contained pressure, of something fiercely controlled. Lifting her eyes to the small figure standing there alone at the end of the room, she wondered what was flowing back with such force into that consciousness? For the withdrawal had been less a withdrawal, Jenny felt, than a strong compulsion toward something else, someone else, perhaps evoked by all the talk about the novel.

The disturbing thing for Hilary, of course, was that she could not approach one element in the past, without raising all its elements, without being assailed by ghostly presences. On the surface she could be quite consciously brisk and analytic, even detached. But under the surface, she was filled with echoes and rumors, with startling images, and the easy talk about the novel had not really been easy at all. Too much flowed back into consciousness. How to separate art and craft from life? How handle all this now before witnesses? She was appalled by the intensity of her feeling, unexpected really, not prepared for, despite her wakeful night. Standing at the window she knew what it was to be in the power of the daemon: there in that summer in Wales, in 1911, the Muse had made her appearance for the first time, and Hilary, the Hilary now over seventy who was also Hilary at fifteen, saw that that episode was perhaps the key to everything. Unconscious of the incongruity of the gesture, she picked up a long silver box, extracted a thin cigar, lit it, and took several puffs, thinking about Phillippa Munn, her governess, who had been the instrument of revelation. They had been sent over with bicycles and knapsacks and told to amuse themselves while Hilary's parents traveled in Spain: as usual she was being "sent away," and as usual whatever pleasure there might be in the adventure was tied down to becoming "cultivated"; Phillippa was instructed to give Hilary Latin lessons, and they were reading Virgil.

Images, scenes, flowed up now. A summer afternoon. They were sitting among the ruins of a castle, looking down on the wide curve of a bay below, munching at huge indigestible meat sandwiches, and drinking cider. Miss Munn was happily unaware that English cider is not exactly like New England cider, and hardly a proper drink for governesses and young girls. The day was hot and rather buggy, and their long skirts were wound tightly around their legs, over high laced boots.

Just below them a young boy was scything a small field. The rhythm of his walk, slow and meditative, his pauses to whet the blade, had a hypnotic effect. For the last half hour they had sat in companionable silence, watching him.

"Why wasn't I born a boy, Miss Munn? It's so unfair!"

"Well, you weren't, so I would sit up, if I were you, and straighten your skirt."

"I hate skirts!" Hilary lay back in the grass, one arm over her eyes. She had the sensation of being inhabited by powers she could not understand or control, a thick mass of electric energy with no outlet, that is how she had felt. "If I were a boy, I would be great—a great poet," she said in a muffled voice.

"Hmph," Miss Munn sniffed. "Nothing to prevent a girl from being a poet, is there?" The disconcerting thing was the complete split between Phillippa's blue eyes and ravishingly pretty face, and the "Miss Munn" whom she put on like armor in her present role. She was not really quite grownup herself.

"Mawkish, milksop stuff! I hate Alice Meynell and Elizabeth Barrett Browning!"

"Why do you, Hilary? You're so arrogant!" Phillippa, like most governesses, was in awe of the establishment, in whatever sphere. Rule number one: you do not criticize your betters.

Actually Hilary had lately learned several of the Browning sonnets by heart, but, confused as she was about her own feelings, she would never have admitted this. She felt it a self-indulgence, like drowning in honey, but this was clearly not to be explained to the simple-minded Phillippa.

"Because . . . , because . . . ," she fumbled, tearing up a handful of grass in exasperation. "Because it's no help, I suppose."

"You're too young to know about love. Of course it doesn't interest you." The most maddening thing about Phillippa was that she refused to rise to obvious bait, and instead, over and over again, relegated Hilary to the manageable world of childhood.

"I'm not a child," Hilary said, sitting up. "Sometimes I feel very old, a lot older than you. Besides," she added in a gentler tone, "it does interest me enormously—, I mean, if I were a man."

"Byron, no doubt?"

"Don't tease. I am being dead serious."

For just a second their eyes met, Phillippa's suddenly flushed with blue as cheeks may be flushed with rose. In the second's confrontation, the pupil in those blue eyes widened like a shutter, and in that second the massive electric current in Hilary connected, so that she felt all through her the explosion of a blaze of light. Then Phillippa withdrew, and asked in a gentler tone, looking off at the bay,

"If you were a man, what would you write about?" Resuming the conversation now seemed irrelevant. Hilary was far too busy absorbing the shock of that crystallizing second when quite suddenly the universe appears to be focused on a single human face, and nothing else exists. She lay on her stomach with her face propped up on her knuckles, chewing a piece of grass, and wondering if the loud thumping of her heart was audible to the magic person beside her. "Oh things . . . ," she murmured, then sat up and asked with a new fierce tone in her voice. "You're such a secret person. What are you really like?"

"I?" Phillippa was startled into confusion. "I'm a rather ordinary person, I guess. Why?"

Something about the coolness, the modesty, the intact quality of the young woman infuriated Hilary. "Because . . . , because . . . ," she struggled for the words, "sometimes you seem to be just a machine for being good. It's horrible!"

Phillippa laughed her gentle elusive laugh. "Dear child, I'm very fond of you."

"Oh fond!" Hilary groaned. "One is fond of a dog, I suppose. I'm a human *being!*" She was standing now and shouting.

"I can't understand why you've suddenly got into such a

passion. . . ."

"Because I love you!" Hilary shouted. "Can't you see?"

"I can see that you're in some kind of state." Phillippa busied herself with packing up the baskets and folding the rug. "It's time we started off, Hilary, if we are to get to Harlech for tea, as we had planned." Was she as bland as she seemed? Did nothing penetrate?

"Whenever you get to be almost human, you have to become a governess again!" Hilary stooped to help with folding the steamer rug, taking care not to brush against Phillippa, for this, she sensed, would have caused an explosion in herself that she was unprepared to handle.

"That is my job, Hilary, after all," she said gently, and walked down toward the bicycles, without giving Hilary a glance.

"Why God should have chosen to make me love you, of all impossible people!"

"I should leave God out of it if I were you. It's possible that He has more important things to think about."

They walked their bicycles onto the road and mounted. Hilary raced off ahead as fast as she could go. She needed to get away from the source of so much feeling to be able to think about it, and to try to control the whirling inside her. Phillippa was quite right, of course: it was absurd to bring God into this, yet she could not believe that the moment of revelation was not a Sign; something far greater and more mysterious than Hilary seemed involved. She felt enlarged by goodness, not an emotion she was used to feeling at all; she would have liked to perform some heroic act immediately, rescue a drowning child, single-handedly put out a blazing fire; she felt like a giant, as if she had grown several feet in the last hour, had grown taller than Phillippa, and so was in some way responsible for her, felt protective and concerned as she had never felt before for another human being. And after a few moments she slowed her furious pace, thinking that the magic person behind her might get tired trying to keep up.

In the two weeks that followed, Hilary emerged from her cocoon, as if she were some awkward luna moth, painfully extricating itself for a first flight into the soft darkness of a spring dusk. She was already then two distinct beings, a floundering physical person who dropped things and blushed and sweated, and a powerful, conquering, violent, inner being who had suddenly the capacity to understand things that Phillippa, the innocent Phillippa, considered extraordinarily mature for age fifteen. Phillippa found herself being quizzed, examined, attacked from every side by an insistent, probing love which was at times disturbing in its force. She felt, no doubt, as if a whole battery of stage lights had been turned on her; it was not a comfortable situation to be in. And she reacted by becoming as impersonal as possible.

"You are so beautiful," Hilary said across the table of an Inn where they were staying near Harlech. "You shouldn't be so humble! You hide, and it's not worthy."

"Worthy of what, Hilary?"

"Of yourself, of what you were meant to be!"

"Good gracious, child, what on earth was I meant to

be?" And Phillippa avoided the searching gray eyes.

"A person, not a governess." In those days of incessant dialogue in which there was no rest for either of them, Hilary had learned a great deal about Phillippa. She was the oldest of a family, all girls, of an impoverished Unitarian minister in Springfield, the only one to be sent to college so far, and she was earning the money now to help her younger sister get an education. Everything in her background had built in the need to serve, but Hilary had dug under that hard crust to the person inside, to the hidden seed of revolt, to the hunger for personal happiness.

"It is very important," she announced, "who you marry."

"No doubt," and Phillippa laughed her haunting laugh, so gentle, so elusive.

"If you marry the wrong person," Hilary said, with the absolute conviction of innocence, "you'll be a slave. I think you should marry a lawyer," she announced, "not a doctor, not a minister. . . ."

"Oh Hilary," and Phillippa smiled a little wan smile, "I'll be lucky if I marry at all."

"Don't talk like that! Or if you do," she added, "talk about being a professor in a college. You are a very good teacher, you know. Think what you have accomplished with me who have no talent for Latin at all!" It was the first time that Hilary had experienced the intoxication, the enlargement of taking into herself another human being, of becoming, as it were, someone *else*. "You are so beautiful, Phillippa, you can do anything you want to do," but now the statement came from power, the power to mould.

"How do you know, dear child?"

"I know because I am often more inside you than I am inside myself. I think about you all the time."

"Where is the waiter? We had better order our dessert," said Phillippa, making the inevitable retreat. And if Hilary was the person in command on these semi-public occasions by the sheer intensity of her commitment, she became a child again after they went to bed. Then it was she who waited for a sign, lying taut while Phillippa brushed her teeth, hoping like a convict for the word of pardon and release. Would Phillippa kiss her good night? Would she show some feeling, even a very little?

Poor Phillippa, seventy-year-old Hilary thought! What pressure she had had to endure! More often than not, she turned her back on Hilary and went to sleep, while Hilary tossed and turned and dreamed of the unimaginable kiss which was never given. And in the morning, Phillippa, refreshed, would see the wan fifteen year old, wide awake, waiting still for the word, the gesture which, within her ethos, she could not, in honor, give.

"What you hope for, Hilary, is not in my power to give," she said once. "And if I did, it would only make things worse. You know that, really, don't you?" And Hilary, knowing it, was silent, only reaching out to clasp Phillippa's hand in an iron grasp.

"Darling, let me go!" And for the "darling" Hilary let her go.

Of course as the two weeks—that eternity—slipped away like a day, the tension rose. Phillippa became aware that Hilary now hardly slept at all.

"You will make yourself ill," she had said once, with real concern. By now, Hilary was hardly eating; food stuck in her throat. She was close to tears all the time, tears of frustration, tears of rage.

"Well, what if I do?" Hilary answered, furious. "Do you think for a moment, it isn't worth it? I know so much I never knew before!"

"Like what?" Phillippa asked gently.

"Oh, *everything!*" Hilary shouted. "You don't understand!" In the grip of the thing, she could not express the multiplicity of sensation it represented, and was well aware that if she had been able to express it, Phillippa herself would have been bewildered and frightened. In the first place Hilary now felt she was two people all the time, instead of one. Her eye had been cracked open by a "you," and she pondered Phillippa as if Phillippa were some extraordinary equation which, once solved, would yield the secret of the universe. But at the same time because of this huge inner reverberation, which stretched all her powers, it was as if the whole outer world also resounded in her . . . landscape, literature, everything had become alive in a wholly new way. Single lines in Shakespeare's sonnets and in Keats spoke to her with such force that she felt they had been written for her alone. Landscapes she had raced through for the sheer joy of riding her bicycle as fast as she could, now touched her like pieces of music and haunted her as phrases from Mozart concertos sometimes haunted: there it was still, that beech tree under which she had lain one day, the silvery bark, crisscrossed with black lines here and there, and the leaves trailing in a watery, flowery way along the horizontal branches; there it was still, that wide shallow brook in a pasture where sheep grazed, and where an old curved stone bridge brought the whole natural, casual scene into focus. . . .

"Everything!" she had cried out, and it meant that if the whole world had become sensation, the whole world had become by the same token, spirit. The totality addressed her, and somehow had to be answered.

"I'm so full of praises and pain, I think I shall burst," she said to Phillippa across the dark.

Phillippa murmured, "Can't you sleep, dear?", gave a little sigh, and turned over; Hilary, wide awake, heard the deep breathing and did not have the heart to wake her. Instead, she tiptoed out into the hall with a notebook and pencil and locked herself into the bathroom: no one surely would want to take a bath at three A.M. Safe, freezing cold, she began to write a poem of her own. And when it was finished, she crept back into bed and slept soundly, for the first time in a week. When she woke, her first thought was not of the magic person, but of the notebook under her pillow and of the work of genius she had produced in the night . . . , oh how relieving to have at last discovered a possible way to use all that had been happening to her! She was not even dashed when, later on, she read it aloud to Phillippa, who managed to regard it in the light of an English lesson and made several suggestions as to how it might be improved.

"But that's the word I like *best*," Hilary had cried out, furious. "You can't ask me to change that!"

They had found a ground to stand on together at last, and the poems poured out. Hilary was allowed to have a room of her own so that she could keep the light on. With a room of her own, where she could pace up and down, say a line over aloud until it sounded right, stay up as long as she liked, and above all feel that the powerful electric current inside her was not being short-circuited any more, the last of the two weeks they would have together, became possible. Everything could now be *said*—this was the intoxicating discovery Hilary made. She could go the limit with her feeling; she could come to terms with it by analyzing it through the written word. She could praise, rage, despair, love, in peace. No one could say her nay: even the self-imposed censor could be quelled. And the result was a series of crude, passionate love poems. Phillippa was shocked.

"How do you know all this, Hilary?" she asked. "You're only a child."

"I suppose I've learned it from you."

"From me?" And Phillippa blushed to the roots of her hair, much to Hilary's delight. "But—but—."

"I've been mining you," Hilary said gravely. "You're a rich mine."

Phillippa laughed her shy laugh. "You are really a strange little girl."

"Why strange?" Hilary asked, feeling dreadfully exposed suddenly.

"You are so self-conscious, so aware of what is going on inside you. It doesn't seem quite natural." And Hilary caught the note of irritation, which she would meet all through her life before the experiential fact that a writer not only feels but watches himself feeling.

"But if I could not stand outside myself and look at myself, I would go mad, don't you understand? Don't you understand?"

"It's disturbing," Phillippa said.

"But all the time I'm myself, I'm somebody else looking on and learning. Why is that bad?"

"I don't know. But it is disturbing."

And so it would be said of her, even into the seventies: you feel too much and you are at the same time too detached to be quite human.

"Why should I fall in love with you, of all impossible people?" As Hilary stood, looking out at the appeasing blue sea, and took a puff of her cigar, that was the phrase that came back to haunt. The sign of the Muse, she thought: impossible, haunting, she who makes the whole world reverberate. Odd that I recognized her at fifteen! And she felt some remote tenderness for that quaking, passionate being whose only outlet had been poetry—, bad poetry, at that!—But who had learned then to poise the tensions, to solve the equation through art.

So intense was the evocation that Hilary felt confused— she had forgotten all about the interviewers. What is this all about? she asked herself. Why am I living it through again? Pull yourself together, old thing, young Hilary admonished. Concentrate! And then quite suddenly it all fell into place, as many little pieces of glass tinkle and fall into a pattern in a kaleidoscope. The pattern was clear . . . , she was still "mining" Phillippa and her own feeling as an adolescent when she came to write the novel; transposed into the very young man and his love affair . . . , a mistake, she saw clearly. But how odd that in the five years that elapsed between the writing of it and the episode with her governess, it was *that* somehow that remained the crucial thing, the unsolved thing, the haunting thing. There the imagination had crystallized, perhaps just because nothing there had been "lived out" at all. God knows she had been in love in the intervening years, the years when sex came to muddy the waters, to bring its inevitable complexities and absurdities. Hilary turned brusquely back into the room. She did not want to be drawn into *that* whirlpool. It was essential that she keep her head.

"Well," she uttered, coming back into the present, coming back to the wing chair and sitting down, "I just had to think something out." Curiously, the five minutes or so had not seemed an interruption to any of the three, and in fact, the continuity was unbroken. "I stopped writing novels because I had the wit to see that for me at that time, it was a false start. *There*, I simply transposed myself. It gave the whole thing an ambiguity. It wouldn't do."

"Why not?" Peter asked. "It did all right for Tolstoy to become Natasha, or for Flaubert to become Madame Bovary." Out of sheer interest, he spoke sharply, but gentled his tone to ask, "I guess I'm being obtuse?"

[109

"Not at all. I have not made myself clear . . . , but can I?" she asked with a little mocking laugh. "For instance, *Rosenkavalier.*"

"Lovely opera!"

"Yes, yes," she said testily. "Of course. But opera is an artificial form, and there this sort of fantasy *works*. It doesn't work in the novel, unless what one wishes is to be Ronald Firbank."

"And you did not?" Peter smiled.

"Oh, I was twenty three and at twenty three one is corruptible. I became the fashion in London. I was nearly spoiled by all the attention I got." She glanced up at the Sargent sketch, her eyes half closed, as if she were daring that self. "I can't deny that I enjoyed it. I made conquests, wore a flower in my buttonhole, and had no idea how silly I was being!" She stubbed out the half-smoked cigar. "Ugh, I really hate them," she explained, "but the doctor has warned against cigarettes."

"And this is your devious way of being obedient?" Jenny asked.

"Devious. . . ." The word hung in the air, then she pulled it down. "Everything that was false in me and in my work at that time was swept away by my marriage. That did bring me to my senses. I was very much in love with Adrian." She turned to Jenny, "Perhaps you noticed his photograph on that wall?"

"A British officer in uniform?" Hilary nodded. "He looks very un-Rosenkavalier-ish, very real."

"Yes. He tamed all the wildness in me, because he was

so wild—killed jumping in the hunting field." But this, whatever it brought into focus as Hilary's eyes narrowed, was to be buried. "He was a great dear."

Jenny, sensitized to these important hesitations, waited for what would come next.

"I never wrote a single poem for him. Odd, isn't it?" She turned to Peter, as if he might have an answer.

"The work of art, you imply, comes from what is *not* lived out?"

"No." Mrs. Stevens lifted her chin and looked over Peter's head into the air. "No . . . I could not say that. No, I could not . . . , lived out on what level, don't you know?" She gave Peter a piercing look. "That's the point, isn't it? Lived out in what way? When does reality grip at the subconscious level? When does reality need to be transposed?"

"I'm frankly at sea. . . ." Peter, for the first time, fumbled for a cigarette. He had been too absorbed to feel the need of one until now.

"But Miss Hare is not at sea, are you Miss Hare?"

Jenny was startled, too startled to think, and she parried, "Because I am sensible?"

"Because you are a woman and a writer," Mrs. Stevens said firmly. "It is a contradiction in terms: men tame women's genius, yet we cannot apparently live without them." She gave Peter a mischievous smile, then turned back to Jenny with complete seriousness, taking her in, taking it for granted that *she* knew all about this. It was one of Mrs. Stevens' charms, Jenny thought, that she never presumed on her age or on her celebrity, never made observations as if she alone had the answer, and even when she was most definite, a question lurked in the background as it did now. "The women who have tried to be men have always lacked something: we have to rest on Sappho, Jane Austen, Colette . . . , we have to be our *selves*. Mr. Selversen cannot imagine what problems that statement might pose, can he?"

"I can try," Peter said, jotting down something on his pad.

"Ah!" Mrs. Stevens smiled a catlike smile. "He does not rely wholly on his memory!"

"It's hard to capture lightning on the page," he said. "But Sappho, Jane Austen, Colette make a constellation. I thought I would just look at those names."

"What do you make of them?" Hilary Stevens asked, not without malice.

"You do it!" For the first time he felt and looked awkward, and Jenny was touched to watch him flounder, he who had seemed always so much in control of the situation.

"Very well," Mrs. Stevens gleamed. "What occurs to me on the spur of the moment—God knows, you are stimulating, you two!—is that the fundamental point is diffusion of sensuality. Colette could write better than anyone about physical things; they include the feel of a peach in one's hand. A man could only write in this way about a woman's breast."

"So?"

"The three writers we have named are predominantly *feminine*—that is their strength. Granted that in Sappho's case, the context was rather odd, but still. Where is all this leading?" she asked Peter with mock solemnity.

"You have brought three fascinating females into the room, but we are here to interview *you*, Mrs. Stevens. Would it be relevant at this point to ask how you explain the change of style in your books of poems?"

"The question is crucial—your questions are apt to be!" Mrs. Stevens answered, rubbing her forehead with one hand, as if to rub out indecision and doubt.

"It is only that I was thinking that your capacity for growth and change is rather out of the ordinary. Probably it explains your triumph this year. Nothing has been taken for granted, apparently. The total opus is a constant re-creation in terms of *style*." Peter laid this statement on the table between them with an air of finality.

"Yes, yes . . . ," F. Hilary Stevens murmured. Then she lifted her head and looked him straight in the eye. "Epiphanies."

"Epiphanies?"

"It is a word, isn't it? Since Joyce. A word with the particular meaning of a moment, or a time of personal revelation, something of that sort!" And she laughed her light, shy laugh, tasting the word with evident pleasure, "Yes, epiphanies. Each book of poems I have published represents the experience of one."

Peter exchanged a look of triumph with Jenny. "Ah! Very well, then let us begin with your first book of poems,

From a Hospital Bed. It was published in 1925, six years after the novel. As the first book of poems of a young woman, it was singular, full of concentrated images, taut, specific, but not a single love poem!"

"They were all love poems, you idiot! All poems are," and Jenny noted that one of those elegant feet was tapping the floor.

"Go to the bottom of the class, Peter," Jenny laughed.

"Well, none was addressed directly to a you." He was nettled and on the defensive, dear Peter.

Suddenly Mrs. Stevens who had looked on the point of getting angry—her cheeks were flushed—relaxed. "By a supreme effort on my part, the 'you' was camouflaged but he was there. The critics called it cold. I have never forgiven that. It was devastating," she said. "It's not your fault—you were not even born," she amended in a gentler tone, "but I felt it at the time. You see, that book was wrung out of something hard to bear. You missed the context: From a Hospital Bed."

"You were ill?" Jenny asked.

"After Adrian was killed in that stupid accident, I waned."

"Waned?" Jenny asked, for the word was startling.

"I can't seem to find a more accurate word. My illness, whatever it really was, was treated as a nervous breakdown—sheer poppycock!—I think now it was some deficiency, thyroid, God knows what. Anyway the prescribed cure was to make me lie absolutely still for a year, not allowed anything at all emotive, don't you know? Personal letters were censored. No newspapers. I just floated there in a cocoon."

"How awful!" Jenny cried out. It was hard to imagine the bundle of nervous energy before them pinned down for a whole year. "How did you manage? What did you do?"

"My mother came over . . . , did she really love me? I do not know, but her duty was plain. Perhaps, actually, she enjoyed herself. For that year she was in total command, and, then, all the doctors fell in love with her, a plain woman with an inexplicable glamour about her, and the voice of an angel. . . ." Hilary Stevens pressed her hands to forehead and let them drop. "My mother read Jane Austen aloud remarkably well. But that isn't the point."

"Epiphany?" Peter asked.

"Oh yes, thank you . . . yes, of course . . . , epiphany . . . ," and once more the tantalizing silence descended. Hilary Stevens bent her head, closed her eyes, and after a minute, the interviewers began to wonder whether she had suddenly fallen asleep. Or had she merely once more left them to chase a hare on her own?

Everything appeared to be quite normal, yet was slightly distorted as in a dream. Had the window of her hospital room really been so huge? She lay on her side looking out at a straggly city tree and a sky where marvelous clouds rose like the breasts of mythical swans She was numb. She didn't even see the clouds, except that the camera of consciousness never stopped registering on one level. She had just heard her sentence. The endless excruciating tête-à-tête with her mother, nothing real or warm ever being said 'because she was not to be upset'; she was to vegetate; she was not to be *moved*, for a year. She lay there, trying to imagine the vacuum, when suddenly she felt her hand taken between two strong, life-giving male hands. It was first, sensation, the sensation of a transfusion of faith, quite impersonal, as if a god had descended.

"I am Doctor Hallowell. I have wangled permission to look in on you at about this time every evening."

"You're an American!" His very intonation swamped her in a tide of homesickness, and of relief.

"Yes. They're short of doctors around here. I thought I might come in handy. It has proved to be a sound intuition." While he spoke, the transfusion of health—of, could it be?—love, poured into her through those warm, vital hands that did not let her go. So schooled already in fearing emotion, she did not dare look at the face. One hand professionally encircled her wrist.

"Pulse steady enough." Then, in exactly the same impersonal tone, he asked, "How do you intend to use this time?"

Cautiously, she opened her eyes, and found herself staring at a queer, almost ugly face, so asymmetrical it was, a bald head with a few white hairs standing up straight on top, and a look so piercing, that she could not have said then what color the eyes were. Later she knew they were blue, very pale blue. They added to the sense one had of a transparent person. She looked, and the tears she had withheld spilled down her cheeks, as she turned her head to the wall.

Dr. Hallowell pulled up a chair and sat quite close to the bed where he could speak very gently and still be heard. "If you will listen, I might talk a little. I can imagine how hard it must be to be stopped, as it were, just now, but most people of your age, you know, are in an awful hurry. And almost never are they given a time like this without pressure. Has it occurred to you that what looks like calamity may be a gift, given to you—just possibly—because you are the rare being who can use a hard gift like this?" Hilary had no answer; she was undone by the tears that rained down her cheeks. "If you could feel," the vital voice went on, "that you are the center of a mystery, and keep your self very still, all may be well. 'The Lord is my shepherd; I shall not want. He maketh me to lie down in green pastures; he leadeth me beside the still waters. He restoreth my soul. . . .'"

"I don't believe it," she murmured.

"You don't have to. I do believe it. One is enough."

In the middle of the institutionalized hospital world where so much was inhuman, so much done by rote, so much mechanical, Dr. Hallowell moved to his own original spirit. Hilary supposed he must be a good doctor from the medical point of view or he would not have been here at all, but that was not the side of him she saw; she was not his patient, but she learned from him what the power of healing is, and how some people have it in their hands;

[117

it flows out of them. What would have become of her there without him? Of course he very soon found out that the one thing she wanted to do was to write poems, and he was able to convince her that it was no punishment but a necessary discipline to lie quite still for weeks. Because he never doubted for a moment that she would do what she wanted to do in the end, she almost believed it herself. And all during that time he was inventing things to make limbo bearable. Sometimes, when he paid his evening visit, he brought her flowers, three roses or a bunch of anemones from the South of France . . . ; that day they talked about the myths of death and resurrection, she remembered. He brought her a book on astronomy, "so you can call the stars and planets, you will see through the window, by name," he said. He brought crumbs in an envelope in his pocket to feed the sparrows on the window sill, and little by little he taught her how to make a cosmos out of the bare hospital room. As if all this were not enough, he managed finally to get up a trio. He himself played the violin with near professional skill; one of the internes played the viola, and one of the surgeons, the cello. On Sunday afternoons, they joined forces to play together. No doubt he had to fight the bureaucracy to get permission for this unorthodox therapy. People were supposed to be upset by music, but if he was asked, no doubt he answered firmly, "Not upset by Bach or Mozart!"

Astonishing man! One spring day when the window was open to the evening air and the sleepy sounds of birds, he had cocked his head suddenly and uttered, "That bird is singing out of tune." He had perfect pitch. And that purely mechanical gift had seemed to Hilary to be a symbol of his being: he was black and white. He was extraordinarily whole, direct, and uncomplicated. At another time, this might have been sometimes baffling, but in Hilary's passive state, it was restful. It was as if he had the intuitions of a highly specialized animal. He could do things that in a less central being would have been cruel, and she could accept them because they sprang from a particular kind of masculine tenderness. He did not agonize: he went straight for the truth. So one evening, as he sat beside her bed, he said in his crisp New England voice, "Miss Gillespie has been taken off this floor. Your job is to get well; you have been getting too involved, Hilary, none of this waiting for *one* person, my dear."

"I wait for you," Hilary protested. She was utterly taken aback that he knew (how observant he was) that she had become attached to Nurse Gillespie, with her austere closed face and clear blue eyes.

Dr. Hallowell laughed. "Your temperature doesn't go up when I am around!"

"The Lord is not my shepherd. I shall want," Hilary said bitterly.

Dr. Hallowell got up and stood at the window, looking out, his hands in his pockets. "It's hard, I know. But in these last two weeks, you have not been getting better. I am a doctor, Hilary."

"But the poems . . . ," she managed to say.

"Keep the poems to objects, not people." He was standing very straight at the window, as solid as a rock. "Look at that tree."

"I do look at it, morning, noon, and night!"

"Have you even begun to see it?" he asked gently.

For he was right, of course. She had not landed in all these weeks. She was still flying round and round in the air, like a homing pigeon, trying to find a resting place in personal feeling. Nurse Gillespie, or someone else, anything except to land on the earth alone, and face it, once and for all. So it had been since Adrian's death, really, a feverish trying to land somewhere. She turned her face to the wall, knotted up into a tight knot of resistance. The life force itself rebelled.

Dr. Hallowell came back to sit beside her. "Now listen to me," he said with great firmness. "What we are trying to do here is to preserve a delicate, an exceptional instrument for registering feeling from busting apart. You are gifted, Hilary. But you are like an athlete who tries to climb Mt. Everest when he hasn't the strength to climb Hampstead Heath. You've got to learn how to handle yourself, woman!"

"I had an aunt who ended up at McLean."

"Well, you're not mad, if that's what you think! But you've used up a little more than your reserve of psychic energy. I can promise you one thing, Hilary. If you get well now, if you learn what you have to learn *now*, you will be safe. And it will never happen again."

"I'll try," she said, but it seemed grotesque that all the trying was to be directed toward *not* being herself, *not* feeling. "But what is it that I have to learn? What is it, really?"

"I don't know." And he laughed. It was one of the strengths of Dr. Hallowell that he never pretended. "But I think perhaps you do. The problem is a certain kind of intensity. Sometimes in my mind I have seen you as a starfish, gripping any hard substance that it finds, as if you didn't *dare* float on the tide. Miss Gillespie is a case in point: there had to be someone for the starfish to attach itself to. For some reason quite beyond my powers to understand, you only feel safe and able to function when you can attach yourself with fierce concentration to one person and not necessarily—this is the point—to someone with whom you could ever share your life on any deep level. Am I right?"

"Someone who captures the imagination," Hilary murmured.

"Someone who starts that whole strange machinery of creation in motion for you. . . . Well, we are in deep mysterious waters, and possibly probing them is not, at the moment, to the point."

"I'm a baby, I suppose," Hilary said, with self-contempt. "Ugh."

"Maybe—but don't forget that compared to a grownup person every baby is a genius. Think of the capacity to learn! The freshness, the temperament, the will of a baby a few months old!"

"And the helplessness, the dependency," Hilary answered. "I find it disgusting."

"Well, you're not a baby, of course. You are far from helpless," and he beamed one of his rare smiles at her. "I'd like to talk a little about the poetry. I feel the greatest respect for your gift, Hilary. Whatever you want to do, you can do."

"How do you know?"

"It's a hunch. Over the years I have come to have confidence in my hunches."

Hilary recognized this positive opening as the prelude to concrete suggestion. So she waited.

"Well, I'm going to dare," he said. "It is daring because I'm not a poet and you can brush all that I say away as irrelevant if you wish, but what if you used the personal feeling as fuel, so to speak, to set the motor going, and tried writing about objects, for a change? Tried, well—I can only think of this in terms of the violin where what I have in mind would be practicing scales—let us say playing with words, for the sheer fun of the thing, playing it as a game, Hilary, with a little lighter touch!"

"Lighter?" Hilary bristled.

He gave her a canny look, hesitated, then said, "I'll stick to it."

Why had she taken it from him when criticism from anyone else was apt to harden her own stance, to make her go her own way with a touch of belligerence? What was it about this man that made her pay attention, that made her humble? Because, she supposed, she knew that he was inside with her, not outside against her. "Bouncing a ball . . . ," she had said to herself. And looking back

now, she saw how huge had been the influence at that crucial time. He had never lit her up as even the briefly contemplated Nurse Gillespie might have, but he did more,
he nourished her. He made inexorable demands. Also he
understood the fundamental being in her. Might a definition of rest be just this, the being understood? Had it ever
happened again in her life, she wondered wryly? Yes, perhaps *once* when for a brief time the Muse was a person
who could understand, as rare an event as a conjunction of
two planets who cross each other once in a thousand
years.

"That marriage of yours, it was all right?" he had asked
once, suddenly red in the face, for this was not the sort of
question Dr. Hallowell asked.

"Yes." She had met his eyes, and wavered. "Yes, it was
love on earth. It was all that can be."

He nodded with instant comprehension. "And you are
one of those who is looking for heavenly love on earth, is
that it?" He nodded again. "Hard on you because it means
hunger and thirst. But you are a poet," he added, "that is
the saving grace." He looked at her quizzically. "But none
of those impossible heavens here, Hilary. Objects, not people, for awhile. That's an order."

And she was compelled by the sheer innocent force of
his person. Objects, yes, but objects described for the keen
ear and eye of Dr. Hallowell. Does one ever write true
poems for more than one person, she wondered?

What she felt, as she sat in the wing chair, her eyes
closed, was an essence. She did not, of course, repeat like

an old record the words, the exchanges, but she felt the presence of Dr. Hallowell again, as if he were standing there beside her, life-enhancing, as if once more she felt the transfusion of faith as his masculine hand took her pulse, as if she were back in the weak, receptive period of the hospital when, for a time, clean sheets on the bed, or a swanlike cloud in the sky, appeared to her with the miraculous power and joy of visions, when, for those strange illuminating months, she was a baby and, perhaps at moments, a genius.

Jenny and Peter had exchanged more than one querying glance, when Mrs. Stevens lifted her head, opened her eyes and said, "You see, in the hospital I had to learn about objects; people were forbidden. That book is the book of a grownup baby exploring every minute sensation."

"I see, but that doesn't explain the technical achievement—babies can't write poems, even grownup babies."

"You learn what you need to know in order to say what you have to say."

"A lapidary statement," and Peter smiled. "But how do you learn?"

"The way a tennis player learns to play tennis, by making a fool of yourself, by falling on your face, by rushing the net and missing the ball, and finally by practice. . . . The point is, partly at least, the intensity of the *need* to master a style, to play a particular game, in this case the game of translating concrete objects, sensation itself into poetry. . . ." She paused, as if startled by her own words.

"Game," she murmured. "It's not my word." She then looked hard at each of the interviewers, as if making up her mind whether to speak or not, and added, having apparently decided to take the risk, "I write for one person, but the person changes."

"The person of the epiphany?" Jenny asked, feeling a tremor run through her, in case it was the wrong question.

"Yes . . . ," then F. Hilary Stevens turned to Peter. "When I said that all poems are love poems, I meant that the motor power, the electric current is love of one kind or another. The subject may be something quite impersonal —a bird on a window sill, a cloud in the sky, a tree, don't you know?"

"But in the hospital," Peter said gently, "you said you were locked away from feeling. Were you visited by an angel?"

Hilary Stevens gave him a mocking glance. "Two angels," she said. "But I'm not going to tell you who or what they were!" Then she amended with a murmur, "May we agree that private life is irrelevant? Multiple, mixed, ambiguous at best—out of it we try to fashion the crystal clear, the singular, the absolute, and that is what *is* relevant; that is what matters." Then she laughed. "I'm being absurdly 'lapidary,' am I not? The trouble is that you are too good, too kind an audience. I find it mildly intoxicating, after all these years, to be listened to."

"We have already been greatly rewarded," Peter said in his most formal manner.

"Well, what next?" Mrs. Stevens asked briskly, as if turning a page.

"What is fascinating, isn't it Peter," Jenny offered, "is that the second book of poems is such a complete new thing, so personal: fifty love sonnets."

"For the second time, at under thirty you broke the mould. That's rather wonderful—."

"Ultra-romantic, self-intoxicated, alive again, I suppose," she said quite fiercely. "There was so much I still had to learn!"

"That's a pretty powerful sequence, just the same," Peter said with conviction.

"Maybe, but I am entombed in the anthologies with that book. And I have grown to hate it—after all it was forty-two years ago, and I have changed." She laughed, "It would be too bad if I hadn't, you will agree?" Then she asked Peter outright, "I would be very interested to know what you see in that book—so old-fashioned, so out of style? Do you really honestly find some permanent value in it?"

"Yes," he said, leaning forward and speaking in little rushes as he did when he was fully absorbed. "What seems significant to me in that book is the emergence of a definite 'I'; the change of style is organic, has to do with the emerging person. You are taking a stance about yourself, about love, your own, if I may say so, peculiar and rewarding stance. What seems to me of value is this stance. Am I way off in thinking that there is something French rather than Anglo-Saxon about this passionate decorum, this insistence on love as a mystique, as a kind of heroic inner demand?"

Mrs. Stevens was clearly interested. She nodded vigor-
ously and waved him on with a smile.

"Granted that this is a totally unfashionable point of
view, I find it refreshing."

"Mmmm," Mrs. Stevens seemed to be humming, rather
like a hummingbird. They could feel her mind darting
about among the flowers Peter had presented to her. "But
did those sonnets seem masculine or feminine, if one can
so define a work of art?"

"I hadn't thought. Does it matter?"

"They are essences," Jenny said, but she was interrupted
by Peter who broke in with great eagerness to offer a further answer to the question. "The style is masculine; the
content is feminine . . . , am I wrong?"

"You frighten me, young man." She turned to Jenny
with an odd little gesture, rubbing one hand in the other,
as she did when she was thinking something out. "Does he
frighten you, Miss Hare? This omniscient being?"

"Sometimes he does," Jenny said. "Then I find myself
hitting back," and she gave Peter an amused glance.

"Quite," Mrs. Stevens paused, opened her two hands as
if she were releasing something into the air, once and for
all. "But there is in that book distortion—inflation—
something that I no longer can entirely respect, the noble
stance, don't you know? The heroic comes dangerously
close to the mock heroic. . . ." She paused and they
waited.

When she seemed to have finished, Peter begged, "Do

go on." His pencil was poised.

"If you will put that notebook away. It makes me nervous."

"But you don't want to be misquoted!"

"I couldn't care less!" The airy tone did not conceal the steel beneath. "I ceased a long time ago to pay the slightest attention to what might be said about me."

"This will not be *about* you. It will be yourself speaking. We are not critics. We are recorders."

"But happily not the recording angel!" she shivered. "Put another log on the fire, will you? It feels cold at this time of day—or there is a change of wind. Soon it will be time for a drink." She looked at her watch, and nodded. "When you live alone you have to have rules. One of mine is no liquor before a quarter to six . . . , although the old need stoking, and once in a while I cheat a little."

"What are some of the other rules?" Jenny asked, feeling a rush of affection.

"Oh," Mrs. Stevens shrugged, "up at seven, some work at my desk every day, come hell or high water, no self-indulgence," she twinkled as if this were a private joke. "Sirenica, my cat, is the self-indulgence. She has to be indulged, you see, as every afternoon she wants very much to be petted and to go to sleep on my bed, so I too have a nap." Then as if this digression had been a short rest in itself, she came back to the subject with a flash of renewed energy. "Now let me put my mind back on your wheel for a moment. I feel I have been evading the issue. What we are talking about is the Muse."

She laid this card on the table, and closed her eyes, which gave Peter a chance to lean forward and give Jenny's hand an exhilarating squeeze of triumph.

"Yes, the Muse has been very much on our minds," Peter said. "We agreed—didn't we Jenny?—in the car on our way here, that the Muse was *the* question. It is wonderful that you are willing to speak of this."

She opened her eyes. "But can I? Is it possible, I mean?"

"May I venture this—the epiphanies you have told us are behind each book—are these actual vistitations of the Muse? An incarnate Muse?"

"Of course, you idiot. Naturally!" For some reason Mrs. Stevens seemed irritated. Perhaps she regretted having broached the subject. She piled up the tea cups and saucers with a busy clatter. "Oh well—," she said half to herself, and leaned back in the big chair, gazing down at them through the mesmerizing half-closed lids. "Graves calls her, if you remember, 'sister of the mirage and echo.' . . . That phrase has an extraordinary relevance to the Muse in question, the Muse of the sonnets." She closed her eyes and leaned her head against the back of the chair. In an instant the life which had been rising through her transparent skin like a wave, ebbed. She looked wan. The dialogue, through which conscience in some form peculiar to herself always reared its head, had evidently been resumed. Neither Peter nor Jenny would have thought of asking a question; it would have been like interrupting a piece of music. But they were taken aback when she suddenly rose to her feet, and stood in front of the fire, to say quite casually, "This is getting rather boring. One reaches a dead end sooner or later, talking *about* these things."

"But we have only just begun!" Peter said.

"You couldn't be boring," Jenny threw in, desperate to recapture the moment of revelation which seemed to have just eluded them. "We listen, as it were, to the Delphic oracle."

"That clever one!" Hilary Stevens sniffed. "*She* never said a thing that couldn't be taken six ways at once."

"You are sometimes not exactly as clear as crystal," Peter said lightly.

"I mean to be." The response was serious. "I mean to be crystal clear—Well then, about the Muse. . . . On that word, perhaps I had better see to the liquor. Mr. Selversen, be so good as to bring the tea tray into the kitchen for me, will you?"

He came back a few moments later bearing a tray holding glasses, a bottle of Scotch, a bowl of ice, and a jug of water, but he came back alone.

"Where is she?" Jenny whispered.

"I don't know. She told me to get out the ice, and I suppose she must have vanished while I clattered about."

"So far, is it going well, Peter?"

"Marvelous, if we can only get it all down! What worries me, though, is that there's a Hell of a lot of ground to cover still. Will she hold out?"

"Maybe drop the idea of each book in sequence."

"What do you think?"

"I think if the Muse is the thing, it doesn't matter about

each book."

"O.K." Peter's head was bent over his pad and he was writing fast. "Maybe we'll have a few minutes now to catch up." Soon they were both hard at work, trying to recapture the word as it had been spoken. How important the silences had been, the expression in the eyes, so piercing and sometimes so remote! How to convey all this? They were so absorbed that they had no idea how long they were there in the great room alone.

Hilary leaned her forehead against the window pane in her bedroom. I'm in a terrible fog, she thought, idiotic. . . . How can I ever tell them? It was like trying to extricate one straw from a tightly bound up bundle, bundle of living, bundle of writing. How to extricate style, the changes in style from the life changes? She felt tension building up; the sweat broke out on her forehead. Not the interviewers' fault of course. How could they know that all this was like an earthquake, throwing up lava and pieces of rock and rubble; the whole past in eruption. . . . Oh dear, it might be a good idea to lie down for a few minutes, flat on her back, breathe deeply, and see if she could stop the whirling sensation, and pull herself together.

But lying down did not have the desired effect, for there, the pressure of the buried memory, making its way up through layers and layers of consciousness, broke free. "I see," she murmured, "I begin to see." But what she saw would never be clear. It had been too strange.

Where and how had Willa MacPherson come into her

life? Odd how some things just dropped out, disappeared, flotsam and jetsam on the stream of time . . . , no doubt they had met through someone in the publishing house where Hilary worked as a reader when she came out of the hospital in that intoxicating year of release, when even waking up in the dreary furnished room in Hampstead was an adventure, for just being alive again, allowed to think and feel, to eat what and when she pleased, to take a bus to Kew on an impulse, to sit in Regent's Park in a deck chair and watch the children and the ducks—when every simple ordinary act of existence seemed like a miraculous gift—and above all conversing with people again, not doctors, not nurses, but her own friends who sat up half the night talking about politics, books, psychoanalytic theory, art, more often than not in Willa's living room on Clifton Hill. Hilary did not have to evoke that room: it was there, the worn comfortable chairs, the two Victorian sofas, the fire in the grate, piles of new books, records, endless cups of tea, and Willa herself with her gray Irish eyes, her wit, her personal style, sitting in the big wing chair. She was, as sometimes can happen, a remarkable person leading a quite unremarkable life, at least on the surface; she did odd jobs for publishers, reviewed for a provincial newspaper, brought up two boys still in school at that time, was always anxious about money, a divorcée. . . . , the frame was ordinary enough, yet within it operated genius of the rarest kind. How to define it? There had been legendary French women, radiant centers like this, critics of life itself, yes, but those women who created salons had been rich, had belonged to a rigid social ethos: Willa had no great house to offer, no prestigious name such as Lady Ottoline Morrell's, the English equivalent in the 'twenties of the aristocrat concerned with the arts. Willa worked hard all day for a living, had nothing to offer her guests but tea and conversation, but the conversation was marvelous, marvelous because of her ability to draw the expert out and enter into his world, while at the same time leading him to explore other worlds; so a young biochemist found himself suddenly conversing with a composer just back from Paris and Nadia Boulanger, and enjoying it. So an elderly, unfashionable woman painter found herself talking brilliantly in answer to Willa's questions, forcing the others in the room to put off their condescension. How did Willa find time to know so much, to be so aware over such a wide range? Of course she hardly slept, was known to read half the night, but it was not really knowledge after all that operated here, so much as a kind of superior feminine power to absorb the essence of a human being. Her poverty, her own hard life gave her, too, that extra dimension, compassion. She was able to elicit confidence. Every one of the men and women who were her friends saw her alone at one time or another, by accident or by intent. The door of that amazing house was never locked.

She was apparently always there for them: in what way were they there for her? Even after all that happened, Hilary never knew which, if any, of those distinguished men who frequented the house, had been her lover. Yet, although Willa sometimes appeared to be an intricate elegant machine, no one could fail to sense that the machine contained a living ghost, that this was a woman, and a woman first of all. How vulnerable, Hilary discovered, by chance.

This is trauma, she thought, as she lay on her bed, reliving an event which had taken place forty years before, and bearing again its difficult freight of shock and revelation. And she wondered whether trauma was not always perhaps experienced when the person most affected was a witness, not an actor, or became an actor only through being a witness of something beyond his understanding. Hilary had come, that day, from a publisher's luncheon in honor of Seamus O'Connor whose second novel was being launched; she was eager to tell Willa about it. What luck to find her, for once, sitting alone in the November dusk, listening to a record, her Briard dog, Gustave Flaubert, at her feet. Hilary flung off her cloche hat, and sat down on the sofa, glad of the few moments left of the Mozart concerto, the interval of listening while the reverberations of the last hours sorted themselves out. There were few rules in this house, but one did not interrupt a piece of music with talk, however urgent.

"I had such a good time with Seamus O'Connor," she began, when Willa rose to take the record off, "such a darling!"

"Is he?" Willa's back was turned as she fitted the record into its case.

"But before I forget, I brought you a record, couldn't resist, I felt so elated when I came out of the Café Royale!"

And she laid the Brandenburg Concertos in Willa's hands.

Willa's expression was strange, as if she was not quite sure she wanted to accept them. She went back to her chair and sat down rather stiffly, holding the album upright, her hands just touching its edge. "I did have these once. Tell me about O'Connor."

"He has bold blue eyes, rather hard, but so bright. Such an edge to him! A ruddy face, in fact he looks rather like a policeman. I liked him because he teased me about my novel, but in such a kind way I didn't mind. And then we talked about landscapes, what kinds we feel for, what moves us. . . . The West of Ireland for him, Maine for me." Reviewing the episode for Willa's ears, Hilary, as always, was forced to evaluate. "I suppose what I enjoyed was the absence of literary talk, for once."

"Will you see him again?"

"I don't suppose so. He's off to Sicily for six months, with his wife and children. But we did have fun!" Quite suddenly Hilary became aware of Willa's silence. That final sentence, "we did have fun" sounded out of key. It hung there in the air between them, curiously embarrassing, while Willa made no response. She leaned her chin on the album. Finally she said, "Let's hear these!"

As soon as the music began, Hilary was aware that the atmosphere in the room had become highly charged. Yet there was Willa, listening as she always did, her chin leaning on the palm of one hand, her eyes looking sideways. How well Hilary would have said she knew that face, but now she saw it as if for the first time . . . the wide brow, a little bombée, under gray hair covering her ears like a casque and parted on one side, the severe mouth, above all the great liquid eyes, eyes which reflected her inwardness as water reflects the moods of the sky, extraordinary eyes which illuminated the intellectual frame they inhabited. Something Hilary had taken for granted about Willa, her always being *present* for whomever sat opposite her in that room, could not be taken for granted now: she was obviously not there for Hilary. And when the vital fugue of the Concerto in G Major began to weave its way in and out, the tension grew so that Hilary would not have dared lift her eyes again, for fear of seeing something she was not meant to see.

She was not alone. The Briard hauled himself to a sitting position, threw back his shaggy head, and uttered a long despairing howl. Hilary remembered that she was relieved by that howl because she suspected this sort of hallucination, but the dog's reaction convinced her that she had not been wrong to imagine that some extraordinary event was taking place. He settled down again in response to a sharp command from Willa, nose on his paws, but the dark eyes still roved anxiously about as if he feared the return of whatever had caused him pain.

At last the record came to an end. He gave a series of deep barks, more like howls than barks—one could only imagine them the expression of relief—got up, wagging his long plume of a tail, laid his head for a moment on Willa's knee, then flopped down at her feet.

If all four walls of the room had fallen in at that moment, Hilary would have felt no surprise.

"Is there an earthquake going on?" she asked.

"An earthquake?" Willa's voice was strained. "You are rather too perceptive." She got up then, pressing one hand to her forehead. "Why don't we go for a walk? Gustav is restless."

Off they went into the dripping mists of the November evening. Hilary walked beside Willa, following her and the great dog who led them both, tugging at the leash. Every now and then they came to a street lamp haloed in light, then crossed through it into the thickening whiteness.

"Before we turn back," Hilary finally asked, "tell me what all this is about, if you can."

"I know Seamus—very well."

"You do?" Hilary felt slightly cheated for having described him in such detail. Then Willa's words flashed again through her consciousness. "Know . . . very well": it could mean only one thing.

"You're a writer, and you might as well know all there is to know about human affairs. I'll tell you a strange story," Willa said. Then there was a pause.

"Don't, if you don't want to."

"I've buried it for ten years. Maybe it's time I told it." She sighed. "A strange story. I was thirty five, he was twenty," she began. "The classic case of the lodger who moves in. My marriage was breaking up. Perhaps we had conceived the idea of a lodger as a way of easing the strain. His presence at family meals would prevent our wrangling in front of the little boys. Seamus thrived on this position, loved having a borrowed family, helped me with the dishes, played with the boys, who adored him of course (you can imagine!), drew J. out about his rare books, was just what we needed, or so it seemed."

"Of course he fell in love with you. I can see that."

"I don't know whether he knows what love is. I fell deeply in love with him, anyway." They walked on in silence. "He's Catholic."

"I suppose he felt guilty."

"There is nothing so frightening to an Irish Catholic as passion in a woman." Willa laughed a hard dry laugh. "It's all right for a man, but a woman capable of passion—that is the flesh and the devil!" Then she added in a flat voice, "He may have had to save his soul, but he didn't have to do it in just the way he chose. No," she said with a certain violence. "He didn't have to do it in just that way!"

"He must have loved you."

"Oh he loved me!" And again Hilary heard the mocking laugh. "He loved me so much that he had to murder me!"

"Even I know that it is the privilege of those who fear love to murder those who do not fear it!"

Then there was again a long silence. When Willa spoke again, she was able to sound like herself, for she said in her usual cool, speculative tone, "We live in a curious age, in an age where passion is suspect. We are lepers. We are treated like lepers. So Seamus treated me . . . like a leper. Worse. Lepers are sent off to their kind to die a natural death."

"And you?" Hilary breathed.

"Burned to the ground." Inexorably Willa's voice went on, to expose what no one but Hilary would ever hear or know. What Seamus had done was to turn up one Sunday at tea time, having chosen an hour when he knew the whole family would be gathered together, bringing with him a young Irish girl whom he introduced as his fiancée.

"What did you do?"

"What did I do?" Hilary measured the strength of the woman beside her. "I welcomed Moira, and I never saw him alone again. Although he had the gall to stay on as lodger for a week."

"What made him do it?" Hilary cried out. "How could he?"

"People will do a great deal in defence of their immortal souls!"

"Yes, but he didn't have to stay on!" His genial laughter, his sensitivity, his humor, his charm rose up in Hilary's mind. How explain such a man? How encompass such cruelty? How do this twisting, torturing thing to the clarity, the light, the balance in the woman beside her? "I don't understand," she said.

"Well, you said it yourself. People who cannot feel punish those who do. It's an instinct like shooting a mad dog. I suppose he would say now that he did it in self defence. . . . He used to call me a pagan. . . ."

Then for a long time there was silence between Willa and Hilary. They walked in the dark, separately, side by side. Out of that long silence, Willa for the first time turned toward Hilary, included her. "It was too strange.

[139

You walked into the house speaking of Seamus, and you brought the Brandenburg Concertos. You see, that is what we had played during those months, over and over again, as if they held the key to everything we were together. Even the dog knew. It was too strange," she said again.

"Yes," Hilary said.

"I was dead, and now I'm alive again."

Hilary experienced something like jealousy before a kind of passion she sensed that she herself would, perhaps, never know.

"Devastating, useless!" Willa added.

"Feeling is never useless."

"I wonder. . . ."

"It has made you what you are. It's why you can do what you do for everyone who comes to your house. It's the other side of your detachment, of your power to include everyone and everything—don't you see?"

"People don't have to be broken in pieces to be useful, Hilary."

"But something has to open people, and it's always terrible."

"How do you know?" Willa asked in almost her usual tone of voice. "You're a poet. You can turn it all into something else."

"Maybe," Hilary said. "But that's not easy, either."

She said it without really knowing. But in the weeks and months that followed she came to know; present when the earth quaked, given to sense the deep tremor, Hilary had been seized by poetry in a new way. Inspiration? It felt more like being harnessed to wild horses whom she must learn to control or be herself flung down and broken. The sonnet form with its implacable demand to clarify, to condense, to bring to fulfillment, became the means to control. Now for the first time she understood about form, what it was *for*, how it could teach one to discover what was really happening, and how to come to terms with the impossible, how it was not a discipline imposed from outside by the intellect, but grappled with from inner necessity as a means of probing and dealing with powerful emotion. From that night on, for weeks, nearly every day Hilary brought Willa a sonnet. Early in the morning, late at night, whenever she could break away from her job for half an hour, she brought one more attempt to contain, to express the long suspended passionate plea—for what? What did those poems ask? To be taken into the flood, to be part of it.

Willa listened. She accepted the poems as the true Muse does with detached, imaginative grace: she brought to bear her critical intelligence, illuminated by something like love, the inwardness, the transparency which had been opened in spite of herself on the night of the Brandenburg Concertos. Above all she succeeded in making Hilary accept that the poem itself was the reality, accept, at least at first, that together, for some mysterious reason, they made possible the act of creation. It was intimacy of a strange kind.

On the surface Willa was exactly as she had been before, witty, cool, the good listener, but there was something—and Hilary was acutely aware of it—that she could no longer control, that rising flood of feeling which had been buried so long. She confessed to Hilary that both men and women among those who had used to come to the house for the good conversation, for the atmosphere of intellectual comfort, had suddenly begun to make personal demands, were drawn to her as lovers.

"What am I to do about this, Hilary? It is so disturbing . . . ," and she laughed. "There's no use telling them I am through with all that. No one believes me!"

Willa had laughed her light cool laugh, but there was considerable stress under it, and Hilary knew that she herself contributed to the stress. The poems themselves denied that Willa was "through with all that." And the time came when Hilary could no longer accept that the Muse must not be involved except as a spectator. She wanted to break through the detachment, through the admirably lucid understanding of what she was doing as a poet, to break through to the woman herself in Willa, to appease the flood with a human gesture. More than once Hilary had crossed the room as if it were a continent or an ocean, taken one of those small tensile hands in hers, and kissed it. At such moments Willa simply waited for the seizure to pass, waited, impassive as some goddess to whom a devotee makes an oblation. There was no human response. But not even this absolute control on Willa's part, this implacable façade, could keep the tension from growing between them. They were being carried on a wave of such depth and force that Hilary could not doubt its reality, and somewhere sometime it would have to break, before it could be sucked back into the deep from which it had come. So she believed with her whole being.

Yet the day came when Willa spoke out sharply. "Hilary, you force me to speak plainly. I simply am not one of those ambidextrous people who can love women as well as men. You'll have to accept me as I am."

"But why does it go on then?" Hilary asked. "I can't believe I am making all this up alone. I'm not that crazy!"

"I can only tell you my truth. I can't tell you yours."

"I feel as if I had been seized by the hair by some angel who won't let me go until, until . . . ," and Hilary had rushed out of the house.

How long had it taken before the wave did finally break? Six months? A year? Such experiences take place outside time, and old Hilary could not remember.

But she remembered that once again chance had played its part, chance or the furies, who are never very far off where human passions are played out. It was after midnight on a spring night. Hilary, on her way home from the theatre, saw the lights on downstairs and walked in to say goodnight: Willa never locked her door. But no one answered Hilary's call, and she had run upstairs, startled by the silence. . . . Was Willa ill, in need of help?

Hilary stood at the open door of the bedroom, in darkness, and heard the quiet breathing of the magic person asleep. For a second she hesitated; it would be kind to tiptoe down and go out of the house, for surely that sleeping, frail humanity needed rest. But who could have resisted such temptation after such months of mounting need? She flung herself down on the bed, and Willa, wakened from the subterranean world where all we control in the daylight lives its strong irrational life, opened her arms to the child, to the poet, to the lover, and allowed the wave to break. Within those passionate kisses sexuality hardly existed, or was totally diffused in a fire of tenderness. The relief of it! The beauty of it! God knows, life had not stopped there when Hilary was twenty nine, but even now in her old age she knew their poignance and their power. She had used the word "trauma" to herself a few seconds before. . . . How could she have forgotten the blessing?

Whatever the psychiatrists may have told us, there are no repetitions. Never again would Hilary experience passion as pure light. The consummation was as absolute as the initial break-through into personal feeling. There was, in fact, nowhere to go from there. And what had seemed to her, as she walked home early the next morning, the beginning of a new life, was in fact, the end of an episode. They did not meet again as lovers.

When Hilary came back two days later, one of Willa's sons was at the door, rather stiff and formal. He told Hilary that his mother had been taken to a hospital and was allowed no visitors. Willa had fallen down the stairs and been found in the afternoon of "the next day" unconscious, with a severe concussion. It had been a stroke, no doubt. John did not ask her in, and Hilary stood there, silenced, trying to read something more in the boy's closed face, hoping for some sign, for some message, but there could be none, of course. She was merely one of the innumerable friends and acquaintances who must be told the tragic fact. She had no right to force her way in. She would not have dared.

Flowers could be sent to the hospital. A ring which Willa had admired in a little box. This was returned a month later, unopened, by John, quite casually and without a word. The boys had been away at school so much that Hilary hardly knew them. On that occasion he stood at the door of her flat, and she did not ask him in. So, twice, they had confronted each other on a doorsill without the slightest contact or real exchange. Hilary was in a strait jacket, unable to move. She went to work every day like an automaton and came back to her dreary lodgings in Hampstead, to limbo. Her desk was littered with words, but they did not connect . . . , the electric current was turned off. What she wrote, if coherent at all, had no form; as poetry it did not exist. After a time she recognized that there could be no relief in merely writing down cries of anguish, and threw it all into the wastebasket.

Three months later Willa came home again and ostensibly resumed her life. People came and went; records were played, but the world that had existed so tangibly no longer existed, because Willa, as she had been, was no longer there. She looked suddenly old and gaunt; she moved carefully and spoke as if she had to plan how to articulate each word and utter it by the force of will. She had never been warm; now she seemed as cold and distant as the moon. So immense was the change that there

[145

could be no question of feeling what Hilary had felt three months before, and never in the years to come did she refer to what had taken place between them. By the time the book of poems appeared, as far as Hilary was concerned, it might have been written by someone else.

Downstairs they talk so lightly about the Muse, the old woman on the bed was thinking. But I can't tell them anything. It is all too strange, too terrible still. Even now, I understand nothing. As she forced herself to get up again, she felt bruised, as if in the last few minutes she had been battling with invisible forces and had been beaten.

And yet . . . , standing now on her feet, coming back to the familiar room, to the warm afternoon light, to the glimpse of tranquil blue through the window, she dared herself to take down the book of sonnets and open it for the first time in many years. It was as if she had never really seen them before, at first too involved in the experience itself, and then finding any return too painful. "After all . . . ," she murmured aloud. After all, the poems existed. That strange marriage of two minds, from which they had flowed, still lived there on the page.

But almost at the instant when she recongized this, she flung the book down, and the everlasting dialogue was resumed. "When did I learn—shall I ever?—that conquest is not the point!"

Peter was writing so fast that he did not hear the light step as F. Hilary Stevens returned to them, but Jenny, lifting her head, was shocked. The old face had gone white;

like parchment, it looked; fine wrinkles which she had not noticed before were apparent. Whatever had happened upstairs had taken a toll.

"We are tiring you," Jenny said, watching the trembling hands pour them each a stiff drink.

"I'm all right," she said testily. "At my age one ebbs and rises rather quickly, that's all. Nothing a drink won't cure!" And she lifted the glass, held the pause a second, and then, sending a gleam of a smile toward Peter, toasted "the Muse!"

"Yes," Peter said rather gravely, "the Muse! Whoever she or he may be!"

F. Hilary Stevens took a small sip of her drink, as if it were some dangerous kind of magic, and tasted it before she spoke. Then she said gently, " 'Whom I desired above all things to know. Sister of the mirage and echo' . . . the Muse, young man, is *she!*"

"So Graves tell us," he answered.

"Yes," Mrs. Stevens now took a long swallow and set her glass down rather decisively. "That is the problem, you see. 'Sister of the mirage and echo,' " she repeated, emphasizing the two final nouns. "It is very exact that phrase; it is prescient."

Jenny looked troubled, and the old hawk caught the look. "You don't agree, Miss Hare?"

"I don't know," Jenny answered, afraid. "I don't quite understand.

"No doubt the problem is different for you."

"I want to believe that a woman writer must be a whole

woman," Jenny said passionately out of her painful sparring with Peter, "and from what you said earlier, what you said about the great women writers never trying to be men. . . ."

"Quite. Hoist with my own petard, eh?" She nodded two or three times half-mockingly. "Well, that's the problem, you see—that's *it!*"

"Must the Muse be incarnate?" Peter asked. "Or is it just a symbol for inspiration itself?"

"Ah, but what is inspiration then? Where does it spring from?" She shrugged her shoulders. "Out of the air?"

"You tell," Peter said quietly. "You know."

"Only for myself," the answer shot back. "Only for myself. Not as a universal rule," and she gave her light laugh. "Miss Hare may be relieved to hear!"

"Is it wrong?" Jenny asked. "You see, I want to be married and have children."

"Yes. . . ." F. Hilary Stevens gave a long sigh. "Yes. . . ." Then, as if she wanted deliberately to break the current of thought, she turned toward the Venetian mirror, "Just look at the light on the daffodils! This is the moment. I placed them there to catch the slanting rays, do you see?"

And to Jenny it was as if she had answered, no man would have done that. Indeed, the setting sun, falling in one long beam on the mirror and the flowers made a kind of explosion, and the two heads which had been bent so intently toward Mrs. Stevens, turned to look. Perhaps this is what the old magician had intended. She sat back in her chair and half closed her eyes. They barely caught her murmured, "There is something ludicrous about women writing these supplicating poems."

"Not Sappho surely!" Peter shot back.

"That was different. Renouncement was implicit, a question of religious belief, what? After all," she smiled half cynically, "all those lovely girls, so passionately addressed and so mourned, were being prepared for marriage!"

"Have we been corrupted by Freud?" Peter asked, with an air of innocence.

"Perhaps. . . . Yes, perhaps we have come to see sex as the devil where actually feeling is the god."

"But we are so terribly afraid of feeling," Jenny uttered on the wave of assent.

"Still," Mrs. Stevens barely acknowledged the statement. "The problem remains. Why can't there be a female Dylan Thomas, for instance? Can you answer me that?" She turned rather aggressively toward Peter.

Catching the ball, he held it a moment in his hands. But it was Jenny who answered,

"The Dionysian woman would be mad!"

"You see?" F. Hilary Stevens laughed. "She knows!"

"Oh," Jenny said with a subdued glance at Peter, "I wish I did!"

Mrs. Stevens let her penetrating eyes rest a moment on that young open face, narrowed them, and said, "Of course, it would be fatal if, at your age, you knew how it would come out, that delicate, difficult, perhaps even harrowing balance of art against life. . . . Life comes first, don't you know? You would be a monster if it didn't."

"By life you mean people, of course, personal relationships," Peter asked.

"Naturally." She reached over and took a cigar from a box on the little table at her side. Peter rose to light it for her and accepted one himself when he had done so. After she had taken two or three quick puffs, with evident relish, she blew a perfect smoke ring. "There, I've done it! I can never make a perfect ring when I try for it," and she looked as delighted as a child who watches a soap bubble float away, but as the smoke vanished into the air, she returned to the theme, "Odd that there has been no great religious woman poet . . . , *that* would have seemed to be one way out."

"Out?" Jenny asked.

"Out of the dilemma of the personal, out of the dilemma of the Muse." Once more they watched the inner dialogue being resumed. She closed her eyes and when she opened them said quite briskly, "But one does not write poems to the Ground of Being."

"And poems are written *to* someone?" Peter asked.

"I think so." Then she paused. "But you make me wonder with your simple questions which are not as simple as they look. Let me leave that question on the table for a moment. What about *Theme and Variations?* Overlooked by the critics, that book is something of a creation." But she quickly withdrew. "Or is that wild statement the effect on an old lady of one strong drink?"

"It's a fine book," Peter said warmly. "I liked it best of all, except for this last one."

"Did you? Did you really?" Her pleasure was delightful to see. It had brought a pink flush to her cheeks, so pale a few minutes before. "I mean, isn't it absurd to care so much? To care really what anyone thinks except oneself and God."

"God?" Peter lifted his eyebrows.

"Yes, God," flashed back. "God as the ultimate arbiter of whether one has exploited a talent or served by means of it, the still small voice, don't you know? Have you never heard it, Mr. Selversen? You are lucky!"

"I've heard it," he said, rubbing his head with one hand in a shamefaced gesture. "I've heard it now and then."

"Conquest or self-conquest, eh?" Hilary Stevens leaned back in the big chair and took a long puff on her cigar. "Self-conquest. In that third book of poems I began to learn something about it, how to transpose, how to be there inside the poem yet outside of it." She looked quite fierce. "I knew the book was good. It was bitter to have it ignored. From then on I felt as if I had been buried alive and was trying to lift the tombstone over my head!" Before either of them could answer, the tone changed. "Ridiculous! It is just as well to have been forced to cut ambition out, to go it alone. I have no regrets on that score. Well, where were we?" she asked a shade anxiously. "You must stop me when I ramble on. . . ."

"Would you like to come back to the craft itself for a moment?" Peter laid down his cigar and took up his pencil.

"Yes, by all means."

"How did you come to remake yourself into the intricate forms you chose to use in that neglected book? To me, perhaps I am wrong, they suggest musical forms," Peter ventured.

"Yes, yes . . . ," she assented eagerly. "How perspicacious you are!"

"And there was a gap of years between the sonnets and this new book. Can you explain why, what happened in the interval?"

"I tore up a lot. It was a time of non-transparency toward life. I fumbled." She came to rest, standing behind the wing chair, resting her elbows on its back, so she looked absurdly small, and more like an owl than ever. "Also I was worried . . . , the struggle to earn a living, don't you know? It was the depression; you're both too young to remember *that!*" And she came around the chair to sit down again, hands folded on her knee with a curiously dutiful air. "My father lost heavily at that time." She shrugged her shoulders. "Poverty is all very well as long as one doesn't starve; but total insecurity is bad for a writer, and at that time I was at a loose end. The wind at my back."

Jenny had the impression that all the above was off the top of Mrs. Stevens' head as if she were tunneling through it toward what she really wanted to tell them. It now burst out in an abrupt sentence, which Peter at once jotted down.

"Intensity commands form," Mrs. Stevens said. "I had lost it. Then it came back."

"How?" Peter asked.

"This is *the* question, isn't it?" She smiled, "And Mr. Selversen's pencil is poised, but I can't possibly give you a simple answer!" She sat there, her hands placed fingertip to fingertip to make a Gothic arch, as if what she were about to utter must be felt out as well as thought out. "Well, it's a conjunction . . . , or if you like, one becomes an intersection. Someone lent me a house in Vermont for two months; the landscape after those hard years in New York did something to me. I felt at home there. Odd, isn't it?" and she laughed her light laugh. "How one does not escape one's roots. All those years abroad. Then a few bare pastures, a rather locked, lonely landscape all told, poor country at best, moved me." She paused. "Also there was time. I had space and I had time. Someone sent me Traherne whom I had not known; I discovered Herbert that summer. And," she dropped her hands to her lap and looked off at the sea, "the Muse reappeared after a long absence."

"The mirage, the echo?" Jenny murmured.

"Yes," and Mrs. Stevens laughed the light laugh which always reappeared like a note in music in relation to this theme, as if there were cause here for a shade of shyness and of irony at her own expense. "The Muse is never wholly absent on such occasions. One must at least glimpse the hem of her garment, as she vanishes into her radiant air."

"Perhaps," Peter said gently, "the time has come to be explicit. Until now the Muse has been very elusive indeed."

"You would have me pin down the mystery?" She laughed now teasingly, a crowing laugh. "But I can't. . . . That's just the point. The mystery cannot be pinned down!"

"You could try," Peter entreated. "A landscape that moved you, time, the discovery of two poets with whom you could identify, I presume, . . ."

"Especially as a craftsman."

"And?" The question was heavily underlined.

"The precipitating presence, I suppose." Mrs. Stevens now looked unhappy, frozen where she had been so free and gay a moment before. "I don't know really that I wish to be probed," she said. But at once the dialogue was resumed, "I might try first in metaphysical terms." She leaned back and closed her eyes. "Let me see. . . ." There was a considerable pause before they heard her thinking aloud. "It is in the gift of the Muse to polarize the poet, to transport him into a state of privileged perception." She opened her eyes again, and spoke out to Peter directly, "Think of a mixture of properties in a chemical test tube: sometimes when two elements are mixed, they boil; there is tumult; heat is disengaged. So in the presence of the Muse, the sources of poetry boil; the faculty of language itself ferments. Does that say anything to you?"

"In a word the poet becomes a lover?" Peter asked.

Mrs. Stevens looked startled. "Well," she granted, "yes,

since poets live in the concrete, the Muse is incarnate. Yes," and she smiled her most elusive smile, "and no, in the sense that this lover cannot live out the experience as it is usually understood, for what the precipitation makes, the new substance, is poetry, not love. They are not quite the same thing, are they?"

"Yeats and Maud Gonne," Jenny offered.

"Exactly. Yeats married someone else. But the Muse was Maud Gonne."

"And there in Vermont, the Muse appeared as . . . ."

Mrs. Stevens waited a second and then answered quite matter-of-factly as if she had come to a decision, "A great singer, Madeleine HiRose. You recognize the name, of course?"

Peter and Jenny exchanged a look, and shook their heads.

"No?" Hilary Stevens gave a deep sigh. Then, as if she were upset about something, she said drily, "Anyway Madeleine had taken a house nearby with her accompanist to prepare for a concert tour. Really," she said quite crossly, "it is too odd that you do not know the name of HiRose. I find it hard to bear." For the first time age had become a barrier.

Peter took the initiative, "Sometimes you are like the Lochness monster, Mrs. Stevens. Now one sees you, now one doesn't. You have a way of disappearing. . . . Come back! Please do."

But the crossness was still there, as she turned on him, snatching at one word, "Oh, we are all monsters, if it comes to that, we women who have chosen to be something more and something less than women!" Then she turned to Jenny and softened, "Miss Hare of course, does not agree!"

"Why shouldn't being a writer make one more human rather than less so?" Jenny too felt a little cross. The question had been aggressive; the answer was sharp.

"My dear child, one is nourishing a talent, expensive, demanding baby! Human? What does human mean? Having time and the wish to care intensely about someone else? This is what women will do, willy-nilly, and what then?"

"But, but . . . ," Jenny persisted out of her own misery, "you seem to be saying yourself that you can't write without love!"

"Love as the waker of the dead, love as conflict, love as the mirage. Not love as peace or fulfillment, or lasting, faithful giving." Hilary gave a strange little sigh. "No, that fidelity, that giving is what the art demands, the art itself, at the expense of every human being." The tone was edged with bitterness, but she added ironically, "Fortunately Madeleine was a sacred animal; she could not be hurt, but what a source . . . what genius she had! And to think you two have never heard that voice, so haunting, so exact!" She seemed to go off on a revery of her own, but suddenly brought herself back to reality with a laugh. "An impossible person, but when she sang she became a different animal. She had an impeccable sense of the exact weight of the smallest word and tone. She could sing a whisper. She could place a shade of meaning on a phrase which made shivers of realization run down one's back." She turned to Jenny suddenly with great intensity. "How do you explain it? The rarity of the artist, the ordinary sensual being that genius was housed in. Even I, even now, cannot bear to admit how awful she really was!" Then she resumed the dialogue. "But that voice . . . , a fountain of life. . . 'Mon enfant, ma soeur, songe à la douceur/ D'aller là-bas vivre ensemble/ Aimer à loisir/ Aimer et mourir/ au pays qui te ressemble,'" Hilary recited, leaning back in her chair, her voice gentled and her eyes closed. When she opened them, she turned to Peter, "What I was after in that book was a poetic equivalent to certain musical phrases, so the villanelle, for instance, with its echos and variations, or the sestina, or even the ode with its long ebbing lines, became appropriate." And to Jenny, "I learned a great deal from Madeleine as a musician, but why is it that women writers cannot deal with sex and get away with it?"

They were taken by surprise; neither could answer.

"Colette, of course, but she is untranslatable into English. How do it in our obtuse language? The language of sex is masculine. Women would have to invent a new language. . . ."

"Did you try?"

"Yes." Pause. "Yes, I did. Thank goodness, I had the sense to tear those poems up." She looked mischievous, delighted with herself. "So Madeleine, though her voice haunts that book, never actually makes an appearance. I

[157

had learned. That was a good book," she added. "I'm glad you think so, Mr. Selversen. As for the Muse," she took another sip of her drink and rested there a moment, "eventually her visitations must be paid for in human terms. And one pays, . . . one is glad to pay."

"Did Colette pay?" Jenny asked.

"Well, I should think so!" Then the dialogue was resumed. "But she was not trapped by her senses. Most women are. There she showed the masculine side of her genius. She regarded herself, I have sometimes imagined, as an instrument for recording sensation, the taste of a Seville orange in contrast to a Sicilian one, the feel of a peach in her hand, so when it came to the big things, she may have suffered, but she kept her detachment—and then she was a pagan, of course, a natural being. Ah!" There was ovation in the way Mrs. Stevens lifted both hands, palms open, on the exclamation.

"It's clear that you identify with this," Peter said.

"Well, I don't know." The hands returned to their thinking position, the tips of the fingers just touching each other, as she leaned her chin on the peak of the arch. "No one brought up in Boston is a pagan," and she smiled, "however much one might wish to be. But there's no doubt that I have always regarded myself as an instrument. That's the point about the Muse isn't it? The moment she enters the scene one becomes the instrument of powers which one does not altogether control."

"So that changes of style are, in a sense, life changes. Is that what you are getting at, do you think?" Peter had glanced at his notes and now lifted his head. "It is such an enormous leap, for instance, from those musically inspired poems in *Theme and Variations,* so sensuously rich, if I may say so, to the book of *Dialogues* which followed five years later, argumentative, passionate," he hesitated, "and perhaps a little dry."

"Damn it!" Mrs. Stevens looked nettled, "I was tired of being so sensitive and feminine! Besides, you forget the state of the world. It was the depression. I was involved, of course. How could one be alive in New York then and not be involved? For a brief time the intellectuals and the political Left came together in a rich ferment. It was rather wonderful while it lasted. One felt responsible." She threw back her head and gave a short bitter laugh. "Things have changed since then." And she added, still in that irritable tone as if, Jenny thought, she were holding something at bay, "My encounter with the Muse was a very hard one, very painful." She seemed about to disappear, but roused herself by an effort of will. "I suppose . . . , really you will think I am mad, and perhaps I am. . . . I suppose I learned through it, and I was not young, remember, that I had to come to terms with the woman in me. A grotesque admission," she said with a short laugh, getting to her feet once more, compelled to walk up and down, clasping her hands together, rubbing them together as if they held a rock between them, as if she were in physical contact with a hard substance.

"Yet the poems are, as you said, rather tough and in a quite different tone of voice to anything you had done or have written since," Peter murmured.

"A watershed," said Hilary Stevens.

Jenny and Peter exchanged a look. She was going to submerge again, clearly.

"There was so much anger, that is what was terrible. Everyone of the poems in that book had to be fought through out of violence, rage. I was sick with it." She shook her head as if she were shaking off leaves or thick fog, and it occurred to Jenny that she had never in her life seen a person in whom thought became such a total process; thinking for this woman was a physical involvement. It added to one's sense that she moved always surrounded by invisible presences. Things unseen were as powerful in her ambiance as anything visible. It made her words about becoming the instrument of powers which one does not control believable, authentic.

What, for instance, now possessed her with such force? She had picked up a small object on the table and set it down hard. "It was a fight for being, my own being."

"Against what?"

"Do I know? Can I tell you?" She wandered around the big table, shifting a book here, a box there with restless uncertitude. "Give me a moment," she whispered. "Give me time."

And before they knew it she had stepped out through the French doors. She had vanished into the blaze. The sun, getting lower in the sky, struck the water and sent back this shimmer of reflected light.

Peter stooped down to take the *Dialogues* out of his

briefcase, and leafed through it. "I don't get it this time," he said to Jenny. "I don't know what she's talking about. It's a queer cold book."

"It's someone else's voice—that's what I felt. It's all a huge effort."

But even with Hilary Stevens out of the room altogether, the silence was charged enough to impose itself. And they whispered.

"It's amazing," Jenny said, "how aware one is of what is not uttered. I feel it a great strain. I feel I am listening all the time to something way below—unspoken—I had no idea it would be like this."

"It is altogether out of our hands now. We are witnesses."

"Has it been like this before?"

"Most writers don't live so near the surface, have more defences. She's an odd one. Terribly endearing, I find."

"A little frightening, I find. There's so much tension. How does she manage?"

Hilary felt huge relief at having got away. She sat down on a stone, letting all that she had held back in their presence flow through her, not trying to control it any more, to be in command. After all, they were used to these absences, by now.

She was forty-five again. How young it looked from here, how old it had felt at the time! She was once more in the presence of the Muse, the crucial one, the Medusa who had made her understand that if you turn Medusa's face around, it is your own face. It is yourself who must be conquered.

"Dorothea," she murmured. And Dorothea was there, conjured up to stand before her in all her cool antagonism and charm. Ten years older than Hilary, at the height of her powers, cynical, passionate, realistic. The anti-mystic by nature and by profession, for Dorothea was a sociologist. The attraction had been immediate, the attraction of opposites. The war had been immediate too.

"How can you turn people into numbers? What truth is there in statistics? How inhuman can you get?"

"You're so incredibly personal. Can't you ever get out of yourself? Must everything come back to *you?*"

They had plunged into argument the day they met at a cocktail party. Hilary remembered how the room had emptied finally and she and Dorothea were still at it, having driven the other guests away with their concentrated violence. I've met my match, Hilary thought, lying awake that night, and I have to understand her. But what she had meant was, of course, I have to justify myself to her. I have to be taken in to this utterly foreign world. I have to be accepted by it. Why? God knows why. She still did not know. All she knew was that she was in the presence of power equal to her own, but in a different universe. And at first she had felt relief. At last she had someone hard enough so that the truth could be battered out between them, inch by inch, no holds barred.

Dorothea was beautiful, casqued in white hair drawn straight back into a knot at the nape of her neck, steel-gray eyes, under fine dark eyebrows, an air of composure, an air of reason which she had fitted over a passionate temperament like a suit of armor. In her outward appearance there was nothing masculine, but the mind was masculine, and the mind towered.

"I'm through with personal relations," she told Hilary the second time they met, for dinner, a week after that cocktail party. "For me, they seem not to work. I have a son. I married the wrong man, and that is that."

"What nourishes you?" Hilary had asked.

"Music, poetry. I work hard and need to be alone when I come back from the office. My students exhaust me." She smiled her rare elusive smile. "I feel I've done my duty by life when I come home after a day of conferences. You've never taught?"

"One, I'm uneducated. Two, it would be a temptation. . . ."

"In what way?"

"Oh, a sort of power, I suppose. Also the quick response—the sense of being immediately useful. You must realize, Dorothea, that a poet *never* feels useful."

"Why would it be bad if you did?"

"It would be too easy."

"I've read your poems," Dorothea said then. "There's something wrong with them."

"You mean you've tabulated them out, put them through the machine, counted the words, and come to this conclusion?" Every hair on her head might as well have been standing on end. But because the person who has created something is always vulnerable, Hilary forced her-

self to listen. Perhaps this formidable creature sitting opposite her was right. But always the moment would come
when all the withheld tension and anger exploded, and she
hurled back her defence, or, in her turn, attacked Dorothea
for an approach to art which remained in Hilary's view,
always just beside the point, just outside the true center.

"The trouble with you scientists is that you really begin
to imagine you can reach all the answers by a method,
some sort of trick, without participating, without being
willing to be changed. How can you approach a work of
art in that arrogant a spirit?"

It was really at first as if they were plunging into a huge
exhilarating ocean, as if the very difference in their vision
of life gave an enhancing excitement to their meetings. Up
to the moment when the anger in Hilary became frightening, frightening to herself, a jinni let out of a bottle,
towering there in the room with a real sword in his hands.

"What is the matter with you, Hilary? You've gone
mad," Dorothea suddenly asked in a dead cold voice.

"The matter is that I want to kill you because you are
the enemy. The matter is that I'm in love, damn it!"

"A strange sort of love, it must be."

But whatever it was, the poems began to pour out.
Hilary walking down Fifth Avenue on the way to her job,
would be pursued by poems, lines running through her
head, lines of dialogue. Day and night, it seemed, she was
struggling like a little bull against a wall, and the wall was
Dorothea. Well, she thought, I have met my match.

"I felt so dusty before you came," Dorothea used to say.

"I really thought I could never be like this again. I feel ten years younger, almost as young as you, if you must know." For she often teased Hilary about the difference in their ages. So for a time, they were lifted up on the spring air, and when the endless argument became too fierce it could be resolved on another level. There was a secret joy when they walked down the street together (for at this time they often set out on long walks) to know that from the outside what people saw was two middle aged women, but inside they were wild children, wild with joy, feeling each of them that this (surely last and best) love affair was a great present from life, a source of renewed energy.

But there was never any peace, that was sure. And the battle became more and more exhausting. What was it really that was happening? What fierce flawed need in them both which flared up into anger, unappeased?

They spent a summer holiday near Ogunquit and for the first time lived together in the same house. Dorothea was the cook; Hilary washed dishes and was the driver and general factotum. There were long mornings of work, long afternoons of swimming and lying on the beach, far up in the dunes away from the crowds. It should have been a time of healing the wounds. And so it began.

"I'm being born again," Hilary felt. She remembered very well waking in the brilliant morning sunshine, watching a light bird on the ceiling, and thinking that she had never felt more womanly since the days of Adrian. Little by little in the months with Dorothea, Hilary had felt the boy in herself backing away, almost disappearing like an apparition, like a ghost who would not perhaps come back again, and the woman buried so long, taking possession.

It gave her immense pleasure to arrange flowers, to make curtains of a lovely soft yellow to replace the hideous ones in the rented cottage. Swimming about in the shallow water where it was sometimes not quite so icy cold, she imagined herself a seal, so sleek and plump and happy she felt. Let Dorothea advance into the harsh waves, dive into them, go flashing off with her strong crawl out into the deep waters where only her red cap could be seen, bobbing up. Hilary was content to stay close to home.

Unfortunately the summer was not entirely one of private lives. Earlier in the spring, Dorothea's study of a mining town in Pennsylvania and of the effects of the shutdown over a period of years had been published. Rather unexpectedly, it was proving to be a great success, and not only in professional journals. She pretended to care less than nothing about a long review in the Sunday *Times*, or about a promised second edition in the fall. All this, she expounded, was quite irrelevant. The study was not intended for the common reader and she couldn't care less. What did please her was the professional response.

Her attitude enraged Hilary, and Hilary was in a particularly sore state because the Vermont poems had also come out in the late spring, and had gone almost entirely unnoticed.

"I'm buried alive. I'm under a stone, trying to push myself out from under a stone, don't you see?"

What mattered not at all to Dorothea was life and death to her.

"I want to be read by people, not poets. I want to be *heard!*"

Dorothea did try to be understanding, but if you try to put a poultice on a wounded bear you get scratched, and Hilary had had a wild hope that at last the critics would come to recognize her, not as a rather old fashioned poet who had started writing eons ago and was still at it, but as someone worthy of discriminating praise in the present. She fought against the waves of depression, the sense of being annihilated, with fierce arrogance. Now more than ever Dorthea's criticisms rankled . . . , and, alas, Dorothea's success in her own field rankled too.

"You don't know, you can't imagine the difference!" Hilary shouted. "The risk I have to take is so much greater!" And later on "A book like yours can't fail, if you've worked hard and honestly, don't you see? We operate from different spheres. Will won't help me. Intelligence won't help me."

"What will help you?" Dorothea asked in her ironic way. "A cold shower and a drink?"

"The gods, the angels . . . , oh you don't understand," and the wild fit of weeping set in again, like a tropical storm. These were the moods of self-doubt when Hilary looked on everything she had written as hopelessly unworthy; then she remembered Dorothea's criticisms and wondered whether after all there was not truth in them.

Then she reacted violently like someone drowning who struggles against the swimmer who is trying to save her. Then she screamed a shrill self-defence which left her afterwards, empty and ashamed.

"You've got to see! You've got to understand what it's like!"

"It might be easier to see if you weren't so violent."

"I can't help it, it's my life. I've staked it all on one thing, writing a good poem, getting through!"

"Well, you just said it yourself, you can't take the gates of Heaven by storm!"

When she was in this state, any opposition, any needling turned Hilary into a dangerous lunatic. Once she hurled half the rented china against the wall. More than once she rushed Dorothea as if they were wrestlers out to kill each other. And if the very violence relieved the tension for Hilary, every such scene froze something in Dorothea's capacity for response, more especially if she had herself become angry as she sometimes did.

"I too seem to be fighting for my life," she said once. "And I won't live in a relationship where I have to become an animal to survive!"

If there had ever been true love it was turning rapidly into devastating, destructive rage. The summer ended in their mutual relief at going back to separate apartments in New York. It had been a costly indulgence in primary emotion.

Would it have ended differently Hilary sometimes wondered at that time, if Dorothea had been a man? And just possibly it might have. But in all this the Muse vanished. The poems stopped. Hilary herself felt like a devastated city after a war. And in that mood she turned away from poetry and wrote her second novel, a novel about the depression years in New York which at the time caused a considerable stir—once more, as with her first, she was briefly in fashion—and left her feeling lost, high and dry. But at least its success taught her one thing: under Dorothea's apparent sense of superiority, under her intellectual approach, there was (it now became clear) jealousy. Sooner or later, oh how those words of Willa's "We are lepers. We are treated like lepers" came back with a vengeance—the creative person, the person who moves from an irrational source of power, has to face the fact that this power antagonizes. Under all the superficial praise of the "creative" is the desire to kill. It is the old war between the mystic and the nonmystic, a war to the death.

Why had Dorothea had to needle her, over and over again, drive her toward those shameful rages, when a word of understanding, a word of *admission* would have brought her back to sanity?

Sitting on her rock, suffering it all again like a single bolt of lightning that shot through her in a few seconds of acute perception, Hilary knew that she had been goaded because in spite of her failures as a writer and as a person, she still was a sacred animal, a kind of totem who must be destroyed for the world Dorothea represented to survive. I was the enemy, the anarchic, earth-shaking power. Oh, we threatened each other at the very source of our being! And very nearly killed each other. It had been too terrible.

But here at the nub of acute pain and sorrow, Hilary lifted her head. Yes, it had been terrible, but we learn most about ourselves from the unacceptable, from the violent, from the mad one who weeps and roars in the subterranean caves: let this one out into the air and he brings the light with him, the light that has to be earned, the light of compassion for *oneself*, the strange mercy that follows upon any commitment of such depth when it is played out and so has to be faced.

At the end we were each broken in half. The boy in me was dead. I had to go on as a woman. And Dorothea? She of the disciplined mind had to come to terms with the anarchic Aphrodite buried so deep in herself, who could not be brought to life except in agony. We were nearly dead; we each knew that this was a final relationship. There could be no other. But we had turned the Medusa face around and seen our *selves*. The long solitude ahead would be the richer for it.

"Oh Dorothea!" Hilary murmured in love and mourning. Then she turned back into the big room.

"I'm sorry," she said, walking back into the circle of the chairs and the fire and the interviewers. "But a great deal has been happening. I have to sort things out. By now that must be clear to you."

She sat down, and clasped her hands tightly on her lap. "What I have to say is this. In a total work the failures have their not unimportant place. You felt the *Dialogues* as dry. Good God, man, they were wrung out of agony!

170]

But I see now that I was trying to use my mind, a big mistake," and suddenly she laughed. "That sounds absurd. I was trying to buckle myself down to hard truths. Perhaps it would have been better to run wailing down the streets of New York, to let the furies out instead of trying to contain them. I got split up, and those poems were the means of trying to knit myself together again. Oh well."And she shrugged. "That book doesn't matter. What I became as a woman and a writer after it, does matter, does seem relevant. Did you think the novel a failure," she turned to Peter, a shade anxiously, "by the way?"

Peter hesitated. He was afraid of breaking the thread. Then shook himself in a queer way he had when he was thinking. "It's good," he said. "You did what you wanted to do. But I think what comes through is your generosity of mind rather than its intensity. One is aware of the effort to do what needed to be done *at that time*."

"Yes . . . ," Mrs. Stevens frowned. "I expect so." She turned to Jenny, "Oh well, after all, Miss Hare, we agree I hope that neither the novel or the poem of ideas is woman's work."

"Simone de Beauvoir— Mary McCarthy," Jenny offered. "Sarraute?"

"Precisely." She paused, hesitated, then closed her eyes.

"Oh please say more," Jenny begged. "It will be off the record!"

"My opinion about these writers can have no interest. I never pretended to be a critic."

"What is woman's work, then?" Jenny asked, abashed.

[171

"Let's explore, shall we?" Mrs. Stevens lit a cigarette and puffed at it thoughtfully. The question was light enough, yet Jenny and Peter both sensed that in the last few minutes, and since Mrs. Stevens' return from the garden, the atmosphere had changed, as if they had all been through a dark tunnel and emerged; they were being included now. And if Peter glanced surreptitiously at his watch, it was because he so feared that there would be no time to reach these further ranges as they opened up. "It is a question which concerned me very much in those years of the novel and the dialogues. I had come through a lot of living toward some conclusions about just this. I was enormously open to what might happen next, to what I might find in me, ripe and ready to be harvested, so to speak. Woman's work?" She half shut her eyes, and she was smiling. "Never to categorize, never to separate one thing from another—intellect, the senses, the imagination, . . . some total gathering together where the most realistic and the most mystical can be joined in a celebration of life itself. Woman's work is always toward wholeness. Oh dear, that does sound vague!"

"Not at all," Peter answered quickly. He felt very tenderly toward her at this moment, and perhaps she caught the tenderness for she now turned toward him with great naturalness.

"I have to place it somehow in relation to men. You see, I have come to understand a great deal through my friendships with men; there, I have been, it seems to me, extraordinarily lucky. I am thinking now of one man who taught me a great deal," she gave Peter a mischievous smile, "at just this time when I was, so late in life, casting off my boy's clothes, emerging from a long adolescence, emerging too from a crucial and devastating encounter with the Muse. All part of the same thing, don't you know?" She stopped a second to gather in a thought. "The problem for an American woman with any real power seems to be that we are all haunted by Thurber's cartoon of the huge threatening and devouring emanation over the house . . . and, alas, it comes too close to the American man's fear of women. Do you agree?"

"They are to be stuffed if possible on top of the bookcase?" Peter laughed.

"Well, you know what I mean. . . . Powerful women may be driven to seek the masculine in each other. The men have been frightened off."

"Your man was not afraid, I take it?" Peter asked.

"Oh!" She laughed, "He loved women. He understood them. Besides, he was French." She lingered on the thought before she went on, then said, looking up, "You know, in those years before the war and during the depression, France became a kind of nurse. We all found our way there—Hemingway, Gertrude Stein, Fitzgerald, MacLeish—because we needed nursing, because we were starved for that deep rich loam. It was not so much escape, perhaps, as finding. Yes," she repeated, nodding her head, "*finding*. You are aware, I presume, that I am about to speak to the point of *Country Spells?*"

"The jump back to your own real voice after the *Dia-*

[173

logues," Peter affirmed.

"Yes. I had been waiting, I suppose, for an epiphany." Once more she half closed her eyes and leaned back in the big chair, as if she were talking to herself, "Sometimes I imagine life itself as merely a long preparation and waiting, a long darkness of growth toward these adventures of the spirit, a picaresque novel, so to speak, in which the episodes are all inward."

This time Peter pounced as she was about to escape into one of her absences. "This time say it aloud."

"Shall I?" She added, "Do I dare?" And finally, "Is that possible?"

"Why not? Again as in Vermont, one senses that place as well as person was instrumental."

Mrs. Stevens leaned forward, clasping her hands in the effort to evoke precisely. "It was a village in the Touraine, high up among the vineyards. It was an empty house lent me by friends. The extraordinary presence who had inhabited it had recently died; I can understand why her family, for a time, decided to lend it rather than dispose of it, for the house had an intimacy, an atmosphere about it so personal, so dyed with its former owner's presence, that it would have seemed like disposing of a living human being. For me, I can tell you, it was a godsend. I came to it, to the silence, to the solitude there, like a sailor who has been buffeted by high seas, who has come back from a long fruitless journey to lie down under a tree, to feel the earth under his ribs again."

"Like Antaeus," Peter murmured. "You had to be

grounded."

But now Hilary Stevens had taken flight, she did not pause to acknowledge him. "I was, I think, only really aware of the aridity of those years in New York when I got away from the city. Women do not thrive in cities. It was wonderful to make contact again with the fundamental business of living, with the vignerons for whom the weather was of paramount importance, a constant subject of anxiety and of discourse, those solid citizens who were still tied to ancient lore. You know," she said to Peter directly, "they will not bottle the wine out of the casks when there is a full moon." And to Jenny she said, "We could talk, you see, about primary matters, the death of a canary or a little dog with a broken leg." Then she was silent for a moment before adding, "I must admit that I was starved, too, for what Luc Bernstein brought me." She lifted her head to ask, "You do know who *he* was?"

Jenny looked disconcerted.

"Vaguely," Peter answered. "One of those French critics —they really do not exist in Anglo-Saxon countries—for whom criticism becomes a *mystique*, who seem to be examining themselves as well as the subject. Someone a little like Charles du Bos. Am I right?"

"I can see that this is not your kind of critic, but you do have the right man."

"I guess we are afraid of this personal kind of criticism. It seems suspect."

"You have to clothe your personal idiosyncrasy in some sort of Olympian pseudo detachment?"

Peter laughed. "That puts me in my place all right." "I only meant that criticism seems to me always personal, however disguised in abstract lingo. Never mind," F. Hilary Stevens said, brushing away the digression. "The point was the man himself, a vision of life, don't you know? A way he had of forcing me to confront myself again, to confront the essential problems."

"Such as?" Peter asked, taking out his pencil.

"Wait! Let me first try to evoke him for you. You are so impatient for The Word, Mr. Selversen, but The Word is always incarnate!" She hesitated after this dogmatic statement, gave him a quizzical look, and added, "or are we once more split upon the feminine versus the masculine point of view?" She did not wait for an answer. "Bernstein was old in 1936 (he is dead now like everyone else) but such vitality! He used to walk over from his house three or four miles away across the vineyards, a pipe in his mouth, a rabbit, cleaned and ready to cook for our supper, in his knapsack. He looked like a peasant in the workman's corduroys he always wore, a soft gray moustache and very black bright eyes flashing out from under an old straw hat. Do I make him clear?"

"Go on," Peter said gently.

"The point is that he was radically himself, fierce about any pretensions one might have: he teased me first about living in such a grand house. The huge forged-iron grilled gate and the high wall around it did give it an air, but actually the house was quite small, a hunting lodge built by someone or other in the eighteenth century, perhaps to house a mistress and thus serve two purposes, for it had a distinctly feminine atmosphere. Luc had loved Anne, the former owner, but of course she was not a poet, and he thought poets should never be rich." She laughed. "He suspected me of that crime, but I soon set him right!"

"You were not rich?" Peter asked with a twinkle.

"Hardly. I had scraped together enough to manage on for a few months, no more." She stopped and suddenly scrutinized Peter as if his question had echoed. "After my father died I did inherit— I sense that you are on the scent—but we lost heavily in the depression. I have never been rich, thank God!" Suddenly she laughed and explained, "That's just the sort of question Luc used to ask me. For a second you reminded me of him, those penetrating eyes!" She half closed hers for a second. "You know, I am not exactly religious, but I believe in fate."

"Because fate has been kind?" Peter asked.

"No," she shot back, "after all, at that time, I was in eclipse as a poet. I was full of rage and hatred. The critics had gone overboard for crude propaganda, as if the so-called literature of protest did not need to be literature at all. On the other hand, those of us who had tried to live out the protest rather than writing about it, were already being accused of being 'prematurely anti-fascist' as reaction set in. It was altogether a nasty time. Never mind," she pulled herself up short. "Let's get back to Luc. You see, I believe we are on earth to make contact, to influence each other, to experience, if you will. People like to believe they are self-made. They are often afraid to admit the influences, either in reality—and then they close the door on experience—or if they are writers of literature itself. I have always been open to influence."

"Most people are afraid," Jenny murmured. "I wonder why."

"There's no standing still. Life at best *is* terrifying, don't you agree? One either keeps on growing and changing (and that is painful) or one begins to fossilize, take your choice! When I met Luc Bernstein I was, I now see, poisoned by frustrated ambition, the ignoble kind. I was already being dropped out of the anthologies. I felt I had ceased to *exist!*" Even now they caught the echo of a scream in the way this was spoken. "In Luc I was confronted with someone as violent, as intransigeant as I am myself. I met my equal in intensity. What a relief! Perhaps he loved me just because I had become so impossible, wild, with all my hackles raised, don't you know? And because he loved me, he attacked. He answered my complaints with that scornful laugh of his, 'and you care what that *canaille*, bought and sold every day in the market of fashion, you care what *they* think!' "

"Strange," Peter said, "that there is nothing of the 'poison' in the poems. The poems are not angry."

"Oh, I hadn't written a real poem for a year when I met Luc. I was high and dry, beached."

"What do you do when you are beached?" Jenny asked.

"Well, I don't lecture or teach, which is what a lot of poets do!"

"Why don't you?" Peter asked. "Is it such a bad solution?"

"I haven't been exactly sought out these last years," she said crossly. "You forget what a dodo you have come to interview!" Then she leaned back and picked up the familiar dialogue. "Am I being honest with you? The fact is that I have lived with the belief that power, any kind of power, was the one thing forbidden to poets."

"Why?" Jenny asked.

"It's the end of personal freedom, for one thing, and the poet must be free to love or hate as the spirit moves him, free to change, free to be a chameleon, free to be an *enfant terrible*. He must above all never worry about his effect on other people. Power requires that one do just that all the time. Power requires that the inner person never be unmasked. No, we poets have to go naked. And since this is so, it is better that we stay private people; a naked public person would be rather ridiculous, what?"

"It has been done, I suppose," Peter mused.

"Well, of course nakedness can become exhibitionism on the platform," Hilary answered tartly. "I don't see myself as a strip-teaser," and she gave a kind of grim hoot. "But to go back to where we were before this digression, what I do when I am in a dry period is to write imitation poems, exercises. . . ."

"But isn't that dangerous?" Peter asked.

"Of course. It's better than taking to drink, that's all. Luc helped me see that it was high time I burned a lot of stuff I had been carrying around like an albatross round my neck. He had an unerring eye for the false impulse, for the willed poem, don't you know?"

"It's wonderfully consoling," Jenny murmured.

"Consoling?" Hilary was suddenly cross. "After I burned the lot, I was ill for days."

"I meant that it is consoling that even you have occasionally hated your own work and burned it!"

The old woman stopped and turned quite gently toward the young woman, "There is so much failure one has to stomach, isn't there? Nausea. Doubt. Anxiety . . . , always and forever anxiety of the most acute kind. How do we manage? I don't know. But the thing about Luc was that I could play it all out against him, with him. We had fierce quarrels, of course, and then a few days later rushed into each other's arms." Suddenly she laughed a merry free laugh. "Oh what a relief it was for me!" She paused, nodded her head as if she were answering a question she had herself asked and said, "Women have moved and shaken me, but I have been nourished by men."

"Yet the Muse is she," Peter reminded her.

"Oh yes, even there, even then. . . ."

"Don't think it, say it!" Peter implored, afraid she would disappear again.

"I'll try." Again she leaned back in the chair and closed her eyes. "It's harder this time because it was all so intangible. . . . I had felt the presence in the house every time I came in again to the dark and the cool after the blazing light. I felt Anne's presence so strongly that it was as if she were there all the time, locked like the small grand piano in the *salon.* Luc told me how she used to sing, not a professional, but there was some quality in her voice that made people weep, 'fresh and passionate,' he said, like the voice of a young girl. One day I felt I had to open the piano and make it sound. . . . I played a few notes at random, then closed it again. I had all the time the sense that in that house music was just on the threshold, until I came to see that the silence itself was the music."

"And then?" Jenny asked.

"Then I began to listen to the silence. Almost without my knowing it, my arid soliloquies, those imitation poems, were opening into dialogue." Suddenly she sat up very straight and clasped her hands tightly almost as if she had made a tangible catch. "It's *that!* When the Muse comes back, the dialogue begins . . . , that is what is meant by fertilization. How extraordinary that I never caught onto this obvious fact until now!"

"Go on about dialogue," Peter said.

"It's quite simple. One begins to talk *to* someone, *about* oneself. Each time one's whole life seems to be in play."

"Yes, but . . . ," Jenny hesitated. "Dialogue means an exchange surely. I don't quite see—."

"Oh, the Muse never answers, that's sure, probably hates Poetry, I've decided in the last five minutes. The Muse opens up the dialogue with oneself and goes her way. The poems of supplication are not the good ones. Do you remember?" Mrs. Stevens asked, revolving her empty glass in her hand, "that some English divine once remarked that it was a mistake to suppose that God is chiefly concerned with religion?" She gathered their delighted smiles and pounced, "So why should the Muse be concerned with poetry? She goes her way. . . ."

"So that silent voice in the house in France, the Muse who couldn't be approached in the flesh, was the perfect Muse?" Peter asked. "What was it about her?"

"Hard to pin down even now. Let me begin with the house itself. It was tangible enough. It had an atmosphere!"

"What kind of atmosphere?"

"Cool and passionate," came the instant response. "Like a note in music, it seemed to me an absolute. In the first place it was rather formal, long French windows downstairs, a few carefully chosen pieces of furniture, which managed to be both elegant and rural. Waxed, octagonal-tiled floors. There was always, as I remember, that sweet smell of wax and burned vine roots. When the evening chill came on, the custom of the house, I was told, was to start the fire with a bundle of dried vine twigs. That made a great blaze; then, when it was really going strong, one put on one or two gnarled old roots or small hard logs. There were several old mirrors in strategic places; they did not reflect oneself so much as the atmosphere, as if seen through water. When the light was fading through the branches of the fir trees outside, there was a moment of rather terrifying poignance. The purity of it all made me feel dreadfully lonely then. There is a difference between solitude and loneliness, as I need not tell you, and people who live alone come to know them both intimately."

"Yes," Peter said, "but do define them each, if you can?"

"Well," Mrs. Stevens clasped her hands together. "Loneliness is the poverty of self; solitude is the richness of self. Will that do?"

"Thank you," Peter said, and quickly made a note on his pad.

"Without Luc's visits it might all have been impossible: together he and Anne challenged me, and in almost the same way, curiously enough. For him she had become, I sensed, a legend, a modern incarnation of the Lady with the Unicorn in the tapestry. She fitted in with his absolute ideas, was capable like him of living in an absolute world, and had bought the house to be near her own deep sources of feeling." Hilary paused to light a cigarette, seemed about to go on, then censored herself. "I am not going to tell you her story. Even now, after all these years, I feel that telling it would be a betrayal. Suffice it to say," she went on with crisp matter-of-factness, "that together Luc and Anne's presence showed up my own chequered life in a pitiless light. Luc hated the complexity, the multiplicity, the ambivalence in me; so I was surrounded in every way by simplifying and unifying powers."

"I begin to see what the word 'Spells' in your title means," Jenny said.

"Yes, I forgot to say that when the dialogue with the Muse is set up, its tangible effect is that lines begin to run through one's head, without the slightest volition on one's own part. Poetry was there when I began to go out for long walks among the vineyards, closed the iron gates behind me, and left the intense, silent enclosure to walk out into the open world, the mysterious, gnarled, ordered world of the vines, row on row, high up on the windy plain, in the distance a few cypresses making their sharp exclamation points against a church tower."

"All this you capture in the poems," Peter said, "yet under them, under the austerity and order, as you put it, I feel a kind of anguish, or tension. One is very much aware that for you the landscape is symbolic. The way the Loire comes back, for instance, the presence of the river. . . ."

Jenny was moved by how closely, how sensitively the young man at her side could participate, so that now when he asked a question, it was almost as if Hilary were asking it of herself, and she answered on the same current.

"I couldn't see the river from the house, but it was always there as a presence like Anne herself. Symbolic?" She raised an eyebrow. "Perfectly real. Itself. Herself. But," she granted, "you're right. There was a tension like anguish. Every visitation of the Muse is disturbing. And here it seemed as if I were being cross-examined, pinned down in a pitiless light."

"Pitiless? All the images you use are gentle ones—a woman seen at dusk in a lighted farmhouse, cutting a loaf of bread across her breast,—that is one I remember."

"Exactly! All these images of rooted human life attacked mine! Anne with her long, faithful, hopeless love, her one love; Luc and his absolute values; a woman cutting a loaf of bread—. Oh," she said with vehemence, "don't you see how they affected me? By their light I had to examine and come to terms once more with my own life. I have not concealed from you—how could I?—that it has been chequered, a life of many encounters, riches, poverty, already fertilized by many people, many landscapes. In the presence of so much wholeness and purity I felt deeply challenged. I had to set something against it. I had to come through to my own source, to my own reality. It was a struggle."

"What did you set against 'wholeness and purity'?" Peter asked. "What do you mean when you say 'my own source'?"

"Oh dear," Mrs. Stevens passed a hand over her forehead, and sighed. "May I let that question pass? I did not sleep in Anne's room, but at that time I used sometimes, before I went to bed, to push open the door and stand for a long time at her window. Swallows made lightning arcs through the air; there was a smell of roses. The evening light over the spacious land. And when I turned away in almost total darkness the great carved bed with its air of desolation affected me like the presence of a huge, haunting dead animal or spirit . . . , never evil and never frightening, only powerful. Oh, I was under a spell, you are right there!" And before they could speak, she went on, "Without Luc, the whole experience might have been too strange, too unreal."

"Did you feel this presence as a question?" Jenny asked.

"Of course. The Muse is always a question—that's what sets up the dialogue." Now once more for a few seconds F.

Hilary Stevens closed her eyes, "And one always imagines that the question might be answered some other way, but it can only be answered through writing poems. The dialogue is not with the Muse, but with oneself." She opened her eyes. "Once I remember saying to Luc, 'Anne wouldn't have liked me. I would have shocked her.'"

"And what did Luc say?" Peter asked.

The answer was that light, self-revealing laugh, "Oh he was kind. He knew a little of the self-disgust I had been suffering. After all, he needled me pretty relentlessly himself. He said it would have been interesting to see us together, the eagle and the dove!" She gathered up the answering smiles. "'Conflict,' he said, 'is your element—what would you do with peace of mind?' He was very well aware, that wise creature, that the Muse destroys as well as gives life, does not nourish, pierces, forces one to discard, renew, be born again. Joy and agony are pivoted in her presence." Then for the first time in nearly an hour Mrs. Stevens got up and began her prowling to the French windows and back, stopped a moment to pick up a Japanese carved ivory mouse and turn it in her hand absentmindedly.

When she came back to her chair, she leaned over the back of it a moment before sitting down again. "I suppose what I really understood that summer was that it was time I stopped borrowing other people's houses, other people's lives, and made my peace with myself in a house of my own creation: this house is the daughter of that house in the Touraine, you see." She came back to the interviewers, sat down, clasping her hands in the now familiar gesture, and looked into the fire.

"All that was long, long ago . . . , and Luc died in a camp before the liberation, just before. No one of us could ask for peace for years and years to come. No one of us could rest, or make a root. The ghosts would not be gentle like Anne perhaps ever again, not in my lifetime anyway. And as for purity . . . ," she shrugged her shoulders. "We were stained to the marrow with something far more degrading and more terrible than love affairs!"

The fire was dying down and the sun, which had momentarily lit up the daffodils, had slipped down behind the rocks. Jenny noticed that the shadow had flowed into Mrs. Stevens' face too, hollowing out the delicate bone structure and giving her for a second the look of a death's head.

"Peter," she murmured. "It's getting awfully late."

He looked at his watch. "Heavens, Mrs. Stevens, it's after six. We are tiring you."

"Yes," Hilary rubbed a hand across her forehead, "I am tired." But instead of breaking off, she sat down quite deliberately. "But the night will come soon enough. Stay half an hour, if you can . . . , if you are not caught here by the ancient mariner!"

"You're incredibly generous. You know it," Jenny answered.

"Not generous. Interested. I said to myself when I got Mr. Selversen's letter that this interview might be a chance to clear a path, to find out where I stand. It's you who have been generous. I've told you things I did not even know I knew!" She lifted the bottle of Scotch. "Well, there's just about one drink apiece left. Shall we finish the bottle in style?" When she had carefully poured out what was left with mathematical precision (that sense of order, Peter thought to himself!) she leaned back in her chair and smiled rather thoughtfully at Jenny. "Miss Hare, would you say offhand that anything had happened here? To you, I mean, as well as to me? Of course," she added with a laugh, "nearly everything seems to have happened to me!"

"Why do you ask me?" Jenny countered.

"Because I should like to imagine that I have been of some use to you, that this exchange has not been entirely one-sided in its possible value. Oh, I am not thinking of what will be published eventually!" And she shrugged her shoulders, as if that hardly concerned her now. "But after all, Miss Hare, wild-eyed or not, you are a woman and a writer, yourself—so—."

"Of course it's been helpful," Jenny answered, "but I'll have to think it all over," and she gave Peter a slightly nervous look. "I mean, there is so much to think about," she floundered. "May I ask one thing, just for me? Not for the interview."

"To Hell with the interview! *We* are important!"

"Do you really think it is impossible for a woman and a writer to lead a normal life as a woman?" But before Hilary could answer, Jenny clasped her hands tightly, for they were shaking she discovered to her dismay, and asked another question, "and must the Muse be feminine? It seems so strange to me because. . . ."

"Because?" The tone was gentle but the old eyes flashed.

"Well," and Jenny felt with dismay the blush rising her throat to her eyes, "You see, I'm in love with a man. I hope to marry him."

"So I gathered sometime ago. My dear child, please remember that I have spoken only for myself. Marry your young man!" she commanded, flushing herself. "After all, *I* married!"

"I'm not afraid, but I think he is," Jenny said, looking down at her clasped hands, afraid of meeting Peter's glance. "Isn't he, Peter?" she asked.

Was there a faint amusement visible in the way Mrs. Stevens turned to Peter and repeated the question, using his first name herself, "Is he—Peter?"

"Listen," Peter parried, obviously embarrassed, "This is none of my business. You two carry on."

"Well, I'll answer," Mrs. Stevens said with a smile. "No doubt he is afraid."

"Oh dear," Jenny said. "I suppose he is. But I don't *want* to be a monster, Mrs. Stevens!—I suppose you think I'm an idiot, but how do I know that I have enough talent, for instance, to take on the full 'motherhood, the full monsterhood' as you put it sometime ago?"

"I don't suppose one ever knows about one's talent. . . ." She paused and closed her eyes, and when she opened them, they were still narrowed like someone looking at a painting, bringing it into focus. "No, the crucial question seems to me to be this: what is the *source* of creativity in the woman who wants to be an artist? After all, admit it, a woman is meant to create children not works of art—that's what she has been engined to do, so to speak. A man with a talent does what is expected of him, makes his way, constructs, is an engineer, a composer, a builder of bridges. It's the natural order of things that he construct objects outside himself and his family. The woman who does so is aberrant."

Jenny swallowed this autocratic statement in silence, but she was frowning.

"Well, Miss Hare?"

"I just don't see," Jenny blurted out. "It seems to me you make art a neurotic symptom, at least for a woman. . . ."

"Oh no," the answer shot back. "Just the opposite. For the aberrant woman art is health, the only health! It is," she waved aside Peter's attempt to interrupt, "as I see it, the constant attempt to rejoin something broken off or lost, to make whole again. It is always integrating, don't you know? That's the whole point. Do you think I am crazy?" she asked Peter suddenly.

"Of course not—but may I suggest that the troubling word is 'aberrant.' What do you mean exactly by 'aberrant'? Who wants Marianne Moore to be a grandmother?" he added with a mischievous smile.

"Well, I don't, of course," she sniffed. "I am too delighted when I browse among her creations. Nevertheless," she turned to Peter quite sternly, "we do all feel, I

think, that we have to *expiate* for this cursed talent someone handed out to us, by mistake, in the black mystery of
genetics. . . ." She paused, frowned, waited a moment,
rubbing her forehead with one hand in a rather nervous
way. "No," she murmured half to herself, "that's too easy.
I've got to *think!*" she said. "Give me a moment. . . .
Maybe it's this: the woman who needs to create works of
art is born with a kind of psychic tension in her which
drives her unmercifully to find a way to balance, to make
herself whole. Every human being has this need: in the
artist it is mandatory. Unable to fulfill it, he goes mad. But
when the artist is a woman she fulfills it at the *expense* of
herself as a woman." Suddenly she relaxed, sat up and
laughed, "So round and round the mulberry bush we go! I
don't make myself clear. I've been too busy doing what I
had to do to think a great deal about this. The interview
—you two *éminences grises* about to invade my privacy
—stirred it all up, and I must confess that in the last few
days I have suffered from rather acute anxiety."

"What made you so anxious?" Peter asked gently.

"Well, I had the curious feeling that I was about to be
found out, or rather that I was going to be forced to find
out something I didn't want to know." She smiled a shad-
owy smile. "That was the attraction, of course. That was
what magnetized, that sleeping anxiety which your coming brought to the surface, not to mention Miss Hare's pre-
occupations, which come back like the angel to trouble
the waters. Why do you want to write, for instance?" She
shot at Jenny. "Do you know?"

"I get filled up. I feel I'm going to burst."

Hilary Stevens laughed. "Exactly! She knows," she said to Peter.

"It's something I *am*, not something I *do*," Jenny went on.

"Well marry your young man with all that you *are*, and see what happens!" Mrs. Stevens uttered, not so much as a challenge as with a gesture of a person opening a door.

"I'm going to have a try—if I can unscare him!"

The darkness had really invaded the room now. They could hardly see each other's faces. For a moment they rested, as if they had arrived at a temporary resolution.

"We have reached *The Silences*," Peter said then.

"Oh that book!" Mrs. Stevens pulled herself up. "Let's have some light on the subject!" She rose and crossed the room to light the lamp on the big table, then one beside her chair. She herself remained standing, leaning one arm on the wing. "The book of this house, the intoxication of solitude. I wish it were better," she said. "It should have been better, and perhaps if I live another ten years, I'll be ready to have another try. But you see, just before I came here, my mother died. . . ." Her eyes were bright. If she had looked tired a half hour before, she was alive again. Feeling flowed through her in a visible stream. And in this curious creature, Jenny saw, feeling acted like light, as if every finest blood vessel which had been opaque, was now lit from within. "Yes," she said, "let us end this dialogue with the beginning. I have sometimes imagined that my last book might be about my mother; it is time to die when one has come to terms with everything. My mother still remains the great devouring enigma, ah!" She came round the chair and sat down, looking at them with triumph, "the Muse, you see. . . ."

" 'Whom I desired above all things to know. Sister of the mirage and echo'?" Peter asked.

"Wait," Mrs. Stevens said. "Let me consider this. Let me try to get there very gently, will you? It is bound to be painful. When my mother died I experienced desolation, and at the same time (this is odd!) a freedom which had suddenly become pointless. Free for what? She was in a queer way *the* antagonist, you see, the one who still had to be persuaded. Of course she had capitulated now and then, to my worst efforts, the novel and the *Dialogues,* those rhetorical arid works. I suppose they did not threaten her. In the ethos where I was brought up, feeling was always the threat," she said drily. "Even art, when in the family, could be threatening."

"You suggest a very repressed atmosphere," Peter said.

"Yes, but," she interrupted herself. "How hard to make you see her as she was! She should have been an actress. . . ." Now Hilary turned to Jenny, "*She* was the woman meant to be an artist who tried to do the right thing!"

"You felt her power?"

"Felt it? Before I was eight it had devastated me, or marked me for a poet. Shall I ever forget that voice reading Arnold's *Forsaken Merman*—'Children dear, was it yesterday?' and the anguish of that cry 'Margaret, Marga-

[193

ret!' I still wake sometimes to that lament, to what I heard in my mother's voice of longing and starvation, wake in tears. . . . Oh well! You see, the hard thing was that the wound she had herself opened was not acceptable."

"How not acceptable?" Peter asked.

"You suggest that your mother *was* susceptible to poetry, to the arts."

"To the finished product, perhaps, but totally allergic to the chaotic suffering, the elements in life itself which make the poetry—totally allergic! Horrified by me as a person after I grew up! No, I had to fight my parents every inch of the way, from the beginning."

"Don't we all?" Jenny asked. "It's the human condition."

"But I loved them; that, too, is the human condition, isn't it? Desperately wanted their approval—so hard to get." Then she added half to herself, "The price of parents! All that guilt!"

"That is not a word you use very often," Peter said.

"I don't use it lightly as it is often used these days," she said sharply. "For me it was a matter of years of arid struggle. After my mother died I did not go to pieces," she said as if she might have. "I didn't because I came and rooted myself here. I see now that as long as she lived I kept fleeing to Europe, and in this sense her death was a liberation. At last I was able to come home and rest my eyes on the sea. Solitude was, for a time, an intoxication; I had been cracked open, and the source was there again. I imagined," and she laughed her light laugh, "for some years I imagined that solitude would be the Muse, that no human being would ever again come to break the mould, but that is another story," she added. "I suppose what I had to accept when my mother died was the hardest thing: you quoted the Graves lines 'Whom I desired above all things to know.' The other side of the coin, I suppose, is the longing to *be known*, to be accepted as one is. Up to the very end, I waited for the miracle, for that epiphany which would open a final door between myself and my mother. Day after day I went to the hospital. Sometimes she wanted to talk, and we did talk, but near the end she asked me whether I did not think of marrying again, and I knew she understood nothing, or pretended not to understand, that she would never, never find me acceptable as I am."

The words lay on the air in a frozen chill of desolation. And no one said anything for a while.

"Is there some connection, would you say, between the constant, recurrent image of the ocean in *The Silences* and some of what you have been saying?"

She frowned, thinking over Peter's question, turning it over in her mind as she turned a cigarette absent-mindedly in her hands before she lit it. "I don't know . . . , do you?"

"Only it's such an obvious symbol, as you use it, for the mother."

Mrs. Stevens sat up straight, quite pink. "Well, you've hit it! You've hit it of course. You're absolutely right! It never occurred to me that that was what I was doing; and the other image in that book is the house—the house and

[195

the sea; I could not speak of her as *herself* (that is what I still have to do before I die), but now I begin to understand what this house is, has been, what it is that gives it for me a particular resonance, why always the silence has been so alive here. It is not that it contains ghosts, but it is in a way, I suppose, a transposed presence itself—how very odd!"

"The Muse, in fact, has any mansions," Peter said with a smile. "We have not talked about the last book, the new one, the one which has brought us and the critics to sit at your feet. But I at least begin to understand what has gone into its making. So perhaps I begin to understand what you mean about 'women's work' too. At least I *think* I do. . . ." He paused and rubbed his forehead with one hand while he glanced back through his notes. "They have to write from the whole of themselves, so the feminine genius is the genius of self-creation. The outer world will never be as crucial for its flowering as the inner world, am I right?"

"You scare me with my own wild hopes!" She turned on him a shy smile. "But . . . well . . . yes, a whole self, the creation of it, and perhaps that has very little to do, dear Miss Hare, with whether one marries or not, strangely enough." Once more Mrs. Stevens held the pause, and they waited for the final word. But she lifted her head then and said simply,

"The interview has come to an end, and you as well as I must begin to feel as if we had made rather a long journey." Mrs. Stevens had become just a little formal, as if she were suddenly shy before the farewells. "Well," she said, as Peter and Jenny rose to go, collecting handbags and briefcases, pencils and pads, "I never did answer your question about changes of style, did I?"

"I think perhaps you did," Peter answered with a smile.

"I shall wake in the night in a sweat, remembering all the nonsense I've talked."

"No you won't," he teased. "Now and then I have had the impression that you broke the sound barrier."

"Did I really?" F. Hilary Stevens asked hopefully. "But I didn't hear any horrifying boom—no windows broken, I trust?"

"I am stretching out my hand through one," Peter said, as his hand was firmly clasped in hers, ice cold he noticed. How well she concealed her nerves!

"And Miss Hare," she turned then a shade anxiously to Jenny, "I hope you have not felt badgered."

The word was so unexpected that Jenny laughed, "For some odd reason you've given me courage," she said, "courage to be myself, to do what I want to do!"

"Have I really? How pleasant a thought, and how did I do that, I wonder? By rousing The Old Harry, eh?" She looked at Jenny quizzically.

"Maybe—maybe because you have dared so greatly to be *your* self."

"Pish tush! You're a dear girl," she said, delighted. "Now off with you both before we spoil this minuet of politeness with some rude word!" And with that characteristic send-off, they found themselves outside the blue door, heard it close behind them as the porch light was turned on, and they stood for a moment, circled round by the unfamiliar dark, in its pool of light, and exchanged a look of understanding and triumph.

Epilogue: Mar

During the night, fog crept in. Hilary woke late to a hushed, milky world, glad to be spared the brilliant light, and to move rather more slowly than usual about the morning chores; even Sirenica felt the change in atmosphere, and had curled herself up in a tight ball in the rocking chair, one paw over her nose. Hilary stood looking down on that pool of peace for a long moment, tasting the silence. Then she went into the big room where it was rather sad and lonely as if the fog had crept in. The daffodils had shriveled at the edges: there was the dead smell of the ash in the fireplace, and bits and pieces of the interview sloshed about in her mind, flotsam and jetsam, not yet absorbed, not yet settled down. It would take an effort to renew this stale world.

"What now?" young Hilary prodded.

"Can't we just exist for a day?"

"Too depressing. Invent something."

"The silver needs cleaning. We could go out and do some transplanting." Even young Hilary was aware that work was out of the question, but the garden, yes.

She pulled on rubber boots and a heavy jacket over corduroy slacks—the comfort of old clothes, the relief of not being "on show" for anyone today!—opened the door, took a deep breath of the chill air, and looked about her.

Amazing how this small world changed in the changing weather. The apple trees loomed up like strangers through the whiteness, their trunks black and sweating. What was so familiar had become mysterious. It might be Japan, she thought, observing with delight the condensation of bright drops of water on a branch of apple blossom. It all seemed to be poised there waiting for a shift in the wind. Very quietly she closed the door and stepped out.

And soon she was on her knees, tearing out weeds, throwing them into the little cart at her side, too absorbed to look up or to notice how often they landed on the ground. Her heart pumped away like a fierce animal inside her. It was good to be alive.

There Mar found her, as he had hoped he would, a streak of mud across her cheek, a cigarette in the corner of her mouth.

"Hi."

She looked up, startled. The boy could be as silent as a cat. "It's you, is it?" Seeing him, a weight fell away, and with the relief of it, she teased, "Well, is it yesterday or today?"

"I went sailing. When I came back it was dark, but that car was still there. They stayed a long time."

"They certainly did, but it was my fault. I got on a talking jag, bent their ears back, I expect. When they left I was as empty as the bottle of Scotch we finished off. But I'm all right now. Give me a hand up!"

She stood there, looking at him. "A good day for a walk on the moors—we might get lost in the fog," she said, "pretend we're somewhere else, in a different world."

With Mar's coming, the tide which had ebbed so low, was rising. She felt actually refreshed; she began to know the relief after a great effort is over. It would never have to be done again.

They walked side by side in a companionable silence, as if that necessary silence were reknitting all the little delicate threads that bound them together, threads that twenty-four hours had torn apart. Every now and then Hilary glanced at the boy, noting that the day alone with the sea had washed away some of the darkness round his eyes.

"Messing about in boats seems to have been good for the soul."

"Mmm," he smiled. "And what about the interview? Was that good for the soul?"

She shrugged. "Yes, I think it was," then threw her cigarette down on a rock, stamped it out, and stood there looking down at it, a frown like a wince crossing her face.

"Of course any attempt to utter the truth about art is bound to boomerang. All I can think of now is all I left out, what a blundering mess I made of it, trying to be clear. . . . Oh well," she turned back to the road, walking fast. "They did really seem to care. No one's come along to ask this sort of question before."

It was Mar's turn to look quizzically at her.

"I found it exciting. I saw things happen right there. Things happened to them and to me."

"I bet they did!"

"I doubt if I said anything very illuminating, all told. But in the deeps of the night, I sensed a book rising. I got hold of something about my mother, a flash of recognition. Oh, they stirred me up all right!"

They had come out to the edge of the quarry, where a smooth-topped stone cliff dropped about ten feet to perfectly still dark green water. The other side, where a few thin birches had sprung up among the stones, was just discernible through the fog, as if drawn in pencil.

"You like getting stirred up," Mar said somberly. "I hate it." He kicked a pebble over the edge and watched it fall and a concentric ripple widen out where it had struck.

"That depends. . . ."

"On what?" He stood there looking down at the water with his intense absent-minded look.

Hilary saw it, but she was also entranced by the scene, by the shape of the quarry in this unreal light. "Poussin," she murmured. "All it needs is a few nymphs."

"Who's Poussin?"

202]

"An eighteenth-century French painter who put imaginary classic ruins down in a French landscape and peopled them with classical figures. You're so illiterate!"

"You can't expect me to know everything," he said crossly. "Besides," he added, thrusting out his chin, "I like to see things as they are. I don't like the idea of those nymphs of yours. The quarry's O.K. as it is."

"If you're going to be cross, let's walk." She had gone quite a piece before she realized that he was not with her, and then turned back, came back to stand beside him, her hands thrust into her pockets. She stood there watching him throw pebbles in one after another, so the circles crossed each other. Finally she stooped to pick up a rock and hurl it into the delicate, interwoven pattern on the surface of the water. It made a great splash.

"Oh well," Mar turned and left. "Have it your way!"

"Sometimes," she said, "getting stirred up breaks a pattern. That can be useful. I admit it's not comfortable, exactly."

"Ugly and devastating," he muttered.

They walked up the road toward the moors, and again let the silence take over. Hilary admonished herself to keep still, for an hour if need be. After all, he had held back whatever it was for twenty-four hours. But she was aware, as they left the dirt road and began to climb a narrow path through blueberry bushes and around boulders, Mar taking the lead, that every now and then he shot a glance at her over his shoulder. What was it he found so hard to tell her now, after all they had exchanged in the last weeks? What harm had come to him?

"I've got to stop a minute, Mar. I'm out of breath." She leaned against a huge granite boulder glad of its roughness and strength along her back. They had been climbing fast. For a second everything blurred, then as Mar's closed face came into focus again, she smiled. There was no response.

"You're always making dark things light," he said, tearing off a piece of lichen and examining it with care, "Things are not clear like you make them."

"What have I made light that is dark?"

"Feeling . . . , I mean. . . ."

"Well, come out with it!" she said impatiently. "What's back of all this? I'm at sea."

Mar crumpled up the lichen in his hand and threw it away. "Forget it." He trudged on toward the moors, his head bent. "Let's walk."

This time there was no drawing together of the separate threads. It was an empty silence. Hilary walked alone behind him, smelling the dank bitter earth smell, picking a laurel leaf to squeeze between her finger and thumb, to breathe in the aromatic sweetness of it, deliberately leaving Mar alone in his separate silence, pretending not to be troubled by it.

Up here on the moors, a wasteland of bushes and rocks, the fog was thinning. Waves of air moved about; every now and then they caught a glimpse of swollen, metal-gray sea below, a thin line of foam lacing itself against taffy-colored rock, and then it blurred out and all was soft gray nothingness again.

Mar had stopped to watch. He offered Hilary a cigarette, lit it, and took one himself. "Well, . . ." he let the word float off, but it was clearly an opening.

"Tell me," Hilary said gently. "Please tell me." For surely this had been going on long enough, and she had to know what was what. "Tell me about the dark," she said. "I'd better learn."

Mar held his breath as if he were going under water. Then it was spoken, quickly in a flat voice. "I went to Gloucester. Got drunk in one of those bars. Spent the night with a sailor in a crumby hotel. When I woke up in the morning, he had gone, and stolen my wallet." When Hilary had nothing to say to this, he added, "Oh, I was stirred up all right!" He imitated her tone with bitter sarcasm.

Hilary knew now that she had expected this. It came as no surprise. But it came nevertheless with the force of shock. She could not like what she had heard. And she was afraid. Feeling his watchful eyes on her, she managed to say, "Well, sooner or later you had to face it."

"Face what?" His voice sounded like a muffled scream. "Face what, damn it? And don't say, 'face yourself'! I'm sick and tired of facing myself. I've been doing that for months, and it's got me nowhere!" He turned on her the force of all he had held back. "You made it all seem so pretty . . . love, feeling, all that hogwash. What do you know about it, really?"

"Very little, I expect," she said drily. "But I have my

ideas."

"Love, wholeness, poetry," he sneered.

"Lust, humiliation, self-punishment. Do you think I know nothing about *them?* Don't teach your grandmother to suck eggs! You make a Hell of a mess, and somehow out of it you learn something about your own inner disorder." The tone was harsh. She could not help it. She was upset.

"Just as I said. You're an optimist!" He faced her now, ice cold in his rage. "That sailor has been sleeping around, and stealing, I suppose, since he was fifteen. What has *he* learned? He *likes* it, Hilary!"

"He used you for what you were worth to him. What did you use him for?"

For a second Hilary took the violence in Mar's eyes. She had seen it once before. She knew how close to the surface it always was in him, in herself too. And she withstood that look and waited. Then, with a bewildered gesture, as if he were waking out of a dream, Mar rubbed his forehead with one hand. His shoulders drooped.

"What did I use him for? A way out, . . . a way out," he repeated in a muffled voice. Then he walked on, picking laurel leaves off angrily, one after another, and throwing them down. Hilary followed in silence, not able to speak even if she had wanted to. She had too much to think about, to take in, to cope with, herself. This was it, she knew.

"I suppose you think I've learned my lesson. I suppose you think I'll never do it again!"

"How did it look to you out there in the boat?"

"Not what you think," he said. Then with harsh emphasis, "I felt starved. I wanted more!"

"More punishment, eh?"

"Danger, excitement, the unknown person—unlike me—conquest by sheer physical need, clean of any feeling except that. I wanted more, I tell you!"

Hilary sat down, not so much because she had to, as because she wanted to stop, to stay put. The moment felt crucial. Just as well, she thought grimly, to be seated firmly on rock.

"I'm not asking for your help," he said. "Get that through your head," and walked off to stand on the edge of an old cellar hole, peering down into it, his hands in his pockets.

Yet he had wanted to tell her, she thought—why? To test the limits? To discover that whatever he did, whatever he might become, he would not be shut out?

Hilary was afraid of her own anger, the old enemy, the irrational power which might at any moment shake her and break through the tension between them, but in a disastrous way. She didn't understand why she felt so angry, why she felt so upset and at sixes and sevens with herself and with him. She would have liked to run away, run back down the path, get right away from Mar and from all he had told her, have a strong drink, read a detective story, lie down and forget it. That is what she would have liked to do.

Meanwhile the silence was growing. She felt Mar's eyes on her face. She would have to say something.

"How much money was there in your wallet?"

"About thirty dollars. All I had. It doesn't matter."

Mar was standing, lowering, waiting like an animal who expects a blow. It came to her then in a flash that he had needed to tell her because he wanted the blow, wanted to be punished, wanted *that* way out of confusion, and she did not say what she had gotten up to utter, something about money, that it did matter, and he had jolly well better learn that it did. She swallowed her anger, standing there beside him and said, slowly, painfully, measuring each word before she uttered it, "Mar, your Hell and mine are different. I had somehow imagined they were the same.

"That was childish of me. But I do know this: people who have angels have devils, and in this we are alike, . . . we'll always be at war with a devil, always to the very end."

"What makes you think I have an angel?"

"Poetry," she said crossly, "of course."

"Don't brush your angels off on me!" For the first time he smiled; the hostility had gone. "Besides, what has lust to do with poetry?"

"Maybe quite a lot. More than we know. More than most of us are willing to admit."

"Why did you say then that our Hells are different?" Mar asked warily. "I don't get it!"

The wind was cold, and she shivered. But she didn't care, now the electric current between them was set up again. Now she could speak out. "Different because you're a man and I'm a woman, I suppose. I wouldn't get any kick out of a prostitute. But I do know something of the excitement of discovering the unknown, how one feels driven to explore the unknown person, to break down barriers, to understand, to be enlarged, to discover, the tremendous excitement of that kind of conquest. Of course sex is mixed up with it. That's sure. But if it were only sex, it wouldn't be worth the candle. When I get stirred up, it's the whole of me that gets stirred. I can't separate soul and body, don't you see?"

"I want the separation," he shouted. "I want to be sexy without all the devastating conflict and *feeling*. I want sex without love! I've waited six months for one word from Rufus!"

"And you can't take it?" she shouted back. "You quail before the conflict. You find a way out, a cheap quick way!" It was a single clap of thunder. After it she asked gently, because she really wanted to know, because he was the strange world for her, and she needed to understand, "Does it work?"

"How do I know?" He pushed both fists into his eyes as if he were blinding himself.

She felt compelled to motion. She led the way this time, down the narrow path, thinking hard. She stopped at the same big rock where she had rested her back on the way up. "I can't see that it works, because you don't really escape feeling. You just get a big slap in the face from it. You settle for shame instead of self-conquest, in other words."

"I'm not ashamed. I'm angry. I told you."

"You were angry when you told me about Rufus. Frustration makes one angry, and that's that. But then you towered in your anger. You were all shining with it. You were ready to battle the universe! I saw you! Oh Mar, this isn't the man-woman difference or even the difference between the deviating person and the so-called normal one. It's life itself. True feeling justifies, whatever it may cost."

"Justifies *what*? A lot of mooning around, dissipation? Rufus and all I have felt for him has held me back," Mar said quietly. "That's what's been so hard all along, being held *back!*"

"Back from what?"

"From college for one thing."

"Oh well," Hilary sighed, "if we're talking about the world!"

"You're safe. You've made it. You don't understand."

"No poet is safe, and no poet ever makes it!" The answer shot back. "If you find it devastating to absorb *one* short episode, consider what it has meant for me these days to try to absorb my whole life, piece together all the encounters—I wouldn't dare count how many!—and try to make some sense of it all!"

"You thrive on it! You're a factory of feeling!"

"Is that how it looks to you?" Hilary pulled herself up from the sheltering rock and walked on. She was furious. She hated the barrier between them which was not really youth against age, nor even masculine against feminine, but quite simply that Mar had not begun to face all she had faced, spoke out of raw suffering, undigested. She had counted, she realized, on essence. It was not enough.

"The big difference between us, Mar, is that you have hardly begun to write the poems. You have been shocked, badly shocked—taking the money was a form of rape, of course. I quite see that. But you seem to be a coward about conflict. You run back to me, whatever I am to you, for a reaction, for punishment, I suppose. Write it out, man! Write the poems!"

"There won't be any poems. Poems come out of self-respect."

"I wonder. . . ." Going down now they walked fast. After a time Hilary turned to call back, "The night before the interview I made myself quite ill, digging out the past, looking at what had fed the poems. Self-disgust! Self-respect is nothing to hide behind. When you need it most it isn't there."

"What is then?" he shouted back. "What is there?"

There was no answer. The wind took the question and blew it away. And it was only when they found themselves back at the quarry side that Hilary, unconscious apparently that it might have been called an answer, totally absorbed in the impression of the moment, said, "Odd, isn't it? How these quarries, blasted open by dynamite, the scene of so much violence, so much lifting and carrying too, after they are abandoned, become magic places, deep ponds." She paused, probing the image which had been spoken before she really saw what she had been given. "Rich and peaceful," she said. "As far as I can see, it's not a question of fidelity, of the violent encounter with no possible future as against some unimaginable lasting fugue. No, what is important is depth. Hell is very deep, as well as Heaven, so we can almost never quarrel with Hell." She looked out over the tranquil deep water, a dark green, opaque, she noticed today, under the overcast sky. How to speak to a wound?

"I wonder whether it is not just possible that you will find that what is not material for poetry is not material for life, . . . too shallow, don't you know?"

"Very pretty, your image."

"A dry quarry is not a *pretty* image, damn it! Bound to be dry, if you separate sex and feeling," she added, glad of her anger now.

"Oh, shut *up!*"

Being angry, it was much more comfortable if other people were, Hilary decided: it freed you.

"I won't shut up! I've got hold of something, and I must say it." She was half laughing now. "You don't have to listen. For years I've been wondering what it is about Europe that nourishes, what it is about *us* on the other hand that feels barren, as if the loam underfoot were shallow, as if the quarries were dry. Look at the faces! Haunted maybe, but haunted by what? Tension, fear, emptiness, self-disgust. Shallow tension, . . . getting there before the light changes! Shallow fear, the fear of being exposed, the fear of emotion, the terrible fear that if you give a fraction of yourself away you are *diminished!*"

"Stop shouting at me," Mar rubbed his forehead in a

compulsive way which she hated. "Leave me alone!"

But she was not to be stopped now. "So we all feel in America. Leave me alone, we say, to be *myself*, unique, untouchable, set apart in my own peculiar constellation of sailors or whatever, of lust and humiliation, repeating the same self-imposed pattern over and over!"

"It's not a pattern for me. It's happened once, for Christ's sake!" Mar was on his feet facing her.

"I haven't finished!"

For a second he looked as if he would run away. Then something in her fierceness, like a small belligerent hawk, its feathers ruffled, touched him. And she caught his look, that fatherly look which she had glimpsed when he first came to ask for the dock. Suddenly they both laughed. The anger collapsed like a house of cards.

"Why am I so angry?" she asked him. "Whatever happened?"

"You seemed about to take on the entire United States, not only me. Here, have a cigarette. Calm down."

"I'm just boiling," she said, "with ideas and things. I'm on the verge of gripping a solid truth." Then she laughed her light laugh, "Idiotic, isn't it, to get so het up?"

But Mar was thinking things over. "I guess you're right. I am afraid of suffering."

She lifted her chin. "I'm not afraid."

"It's all grist to your mill. Even the Hell gets to be useful."

"Yes." She questioned his face, no longer open nor smiling. "If you find that disgusting, you're not a writer."

"It seems like rather an easy way out."

"*Easy?*" She turned on him sharply. "Easy?" she repeated. "It's not a way out at all; it's a way *in*—excruciating self-discipline, the ability to deal with anxiety, the
need to transpose from one plane of reality to another, the
fighting through each time to the *means* toward this
transposition. Easy?" She flashed out again. "A way out?
That's not fair. It's rather more costly than *your* way out
two nights ago, I can tell you!"

"Leave me out of it. Talk to yourself," Mar said quietly.

"That's what I'm doing, you idiot . . . talking to myself, whistling in the dark." The words she had uttered
spontaneously reverberated. "Talking to myself. . . ."

It was true. Mar was a buried part of herself. Mar was
the young man she had dreamed of being. That was why
the episode of the sailor had been so disturbing, had jarred
her at some deep level of consciousness, had almost split
her off from him into that dangerous anger so much like
pain. Turn that troubled, troubling face around and it was
her own face.

"Everyone is everyone," she murmured. "Only you and I
are more so."

Mar had walked away, was standing a little distance
away, not throwing pebbles in to trouble the waters this
time, just standing there. And she too looked down into
the deep still pool, as if he were not there, and she could
rest for a moment on nature itself. It was very still, and in
the stillness she became excruciatingly aware of what
might lie ahead for him, of the danger he was in, of the

danger of her way of taking life, of battling through suffering, of taking on suffering almost with joy, of using deprivation as a springboard into poetry. Did he have enough talent? A hard enough core? Would he be drowned in the winds and the tides, tossed up and down, never coming to shore? She was deeply frightened. She saw that she had been saved a great deal by being a woman, been saved by nature itself from some kinds of degradation and shame, and that she had been saved also by being a mystic of sorts. Transcending, sublimating—these would not be his way. His way would have to deal with gritty substance; the quarry as it was, not seen in a special light. He must not be bound to her wheel of boy and woman and the two married within her to make the poems. His poems would be cramped and distorted if he did not live out his life to the full, as a man. And she was afraid because of all she had told him, asked of him, believed could be possible for him, as if he were herself. Here she ground her teeth to keep from swearing aloud, so fierce was her sense of failure in regard to him. He must have a whole life, grow up, marry. So she knew in the very center of her being. How to set him free? How persuade?

"I'm an old woman, Mar. You must grant me that."

"Do I have to?" He came back toward her, smiling. "You talk about it a lot, but you don't seem exactly old. Or young either. Just yourself," he said considering her with evident pleasure.

"I've *earned* being old," she said. "Don't deprive me of what I have earned."

"Well?"

"First, there are no casual encounters, for you or for me. Every one is a collision, reverberates, and, because it reverberates, is costly."

"What has our collision cost you?"

"A home truth," she said quietly. "Never mind that for the moment. The wonderful thing that happened when we collided was poetry. That's true. You can't deny it."

"I wouldn't think of denying it."

"You stirred me up. The old machine got into gear again, don't you know? You were stirred up anyway, and all I had to do was discover you had a secret weapon, a talent. It has been exciting, Mar, hasn't it?" She didn't wait for an answer. "Something else happened which I am only beginning to understand." Catching his amused look, his fatherly look, Hilary was dismayed. It was all going to be harder than she knew quite how to manage. "You're not going to like it!" she said with an edge in her voice. But oh be gentle, something warned her. Summon your gentleness now. (And from somewhere deep down she heard Margaret's voice, so long ago, saying about Adrian, "Life with Adrian is going to ask all your tenderness, all your womanliness.")

Mar was at this moment swinging a birch branch down, feeling his strength against the limber strength of the tree, letting it snap back and take him part way with it.

"Hilary has one more thing to say, and I'm not going to like it. Well?" And he let the branch go, watched it spring back. "What is it, Hilary?" He stood there with his hands in his pockets, daring her. For the first time that morning, the shadow of the sailor was not standing behind him. His eyes looked very blue, and for a second Hilary envied him, envied that masculine power, that youth, the *animal* in him.

"I'm an old woman," she said heavily, and this time with disgust. "But when I was your age, or a little younger maybe, I wanted to be a boy. Part of me just stayed back there, and you can laugh if you must—it might be appropriate!—but it was (and *is*) that boy in me who wrote the poems. So I have kept him close to me, for better or worse, and perhaps justified my way of life in the light of his immature eyes."

Mar was dead serious now. "Do you really think," he asked, "that the poems are immature?"

"Sit down beside me, will you? It makes me nervous having you stand there like a father-figure looming over me."

Obediently Mar sat down, cross-legged, beside her. "You flatter me," he said.

"I don't flatter. I saw the father-figure the first day you appeared out of the blue, asked for my dock, and said that since I had no one to help me, you guessed you would have to carry in wood and do the odd jobs. I'm afraid, dear Mar, that it was the fatherliness which touched my iron heart."

"I don't know about the boy in you," Mar said. "I only know about the woman." Then he added with an ironic smile, "As for myself, I don't know about the father. I only know about the boy." Then he added, serious, "But you haven't answered my question about your poems."

"Very well. I'll answer it. They are not immature. But they have been too costly. By that I mean that they might have been warmer and richer if I had not chosen the path I did choose, the path of transcendence, the path of the impossible transcended. Mar, I have asked a great deal of myself, I wonder whether it was necessary. I'm at the end of a long life of beating my head against the wall of myself. You are at the beginning. It seems absurd to consider that you have been deeply in love, just once, just *once*," she said fiercely.

"What's wrong with that?"

"Nothing. It's bitten you like a talent. Ah," she added, catching his look, "it is the talent for poetry, this talent for love, and no true poetry without it. Why? Because it's the talent for going naked. When you told me about Rufus, you had no skin. You were an orphan. I saw poetry as the way of helping you grow a skin. Give me a light!" she commanded.

"Are you trying to tell me that you were lying?" She saw that his hand was trembling as he lit her cigarette. "You mean I have no talent? The poems you got me to write were just some kind of poultice on a wound? Is that what you have to say?"

"No, you fool!" She was exasperated by the misunderstanding, so radical and so unexpected. "It's just because I feel your talent, real and gritty and uncompromising, a *masculine* talent, that I came to see just now that I could do you harm, not good, that I could be the short-circuit for you in the long run. Everything I said about you and Rufus, I meant. If this thing about Rufus broke through into the place of poetry for you, so much the better. If this was your path inwards, so much the better. If one un- happy homosexual experience taught you what you might become, all to the good. But if one dirty night with a sailor who stole your wallet makes you think this is your real life, Mar, you're going to be in the fruitless Hell. You have to go on as a man, not a boy, don't you see?"

"You see me, do you, as a husband and a father?"

For a second they confronted each other, the bold blue eyes of Mar and the hooded gray eyes of Hilary. Then at the same instant, each reached for a pebble and threw it down. The two pebbles struck the water about two feet apart, and they watched avidly as the two great widening ripples intersected. In the stillness of the quarry water, it was amazing what a dramatic effect it had.

"Somehow," Hilary murmured, "I see your collisions as fruitful outside the poems. I would wish you happiness." Rather clumsily she lifted herself to her feet. "For you it does not seem to me an impossible wish."

"Mmmm." Mar sat there, hugging his knees. "You mean," and he looked up at her quizzically, "you would have liked to be a husband and father, so I've got to be?"

For a second they balanced there on the brink of laugh- ter. But Hilary was serious when she answered, "No, I think I would have liked to be a woman, simple and fruit- ful, a woman with many children, a great husband, . . . and no talent!"

"You see," he frowned, "the talent always comes in, like a red herring. There is no escaping *it!*"

And he was on his feet.

"Life and a talent, . . . I wonder." She leaned one hand on his shoulder, and they walked away from the quarry together. In the distance at the end of the road, she could see the house, the blue door caught in the sunlight. Peace and order, she thought. Peace, order, and poetry, to be won over and over again, and never for good, out of the raw, chaotic material. Nothing really mattered now except to get back to her study, to slip a white sheet of paper into the typewriter, to begin again from here.

"All I meant to say, Mar, is that every end is a beginning."